I

MW01196200

Dune House Cozy Mystery Series

Cindy Bell

ISBN-13: 978-1503216235

ISBN-10: 1503216233

More Cozy Mysteries by Cindy Bell

Dune House Cozy Mystery Series

Seaside Secrets

Boats and Bad Guys

Treasured History

Hidden Hideaways

Heavenly Highland Inn Cozy Mystery Series

Murdering the Roses

Dead in the Daisies

Killing the Carnations

Drowning the Daffodils

Suffocating the Sunflowers

Books, Bullets and Blooms

A Deadly serious Gardening Contest

Wendy the Wedding Planner Cozy Mystery Series

Matrimony, Money and Murder

Chefs, Ceremonies and Crimes

Bekki the Beautician Cozy Mystery Series

Hairspray and Homicide

A Dyed Blonde and a Dead Body

Mascara and Murder

Pageant and Poison

Conditioner and a Corpse

Mistletoe, Makeup and Murder

Hairpin, Hair Dryer and Homicide

Blush, a Bride and a Body

Shampoo and a Stiff

Cosmetics, a Cruise and a Killer

Lipstick, a Long Iron and Lifeless

Camping, Concealer and Criminals

Table of Contents

Chapter One

"Wait, don't!" Paul pleaded as he backed up across the sand. His eyes were wide with fear, and his hands were held out before him protectively.

"I'm sorry, Paul," Suzie said as she tried to keep her voice calm. "But you asked for this. Now, you're going to have to accept the consequences."

"Only if you can catch me!" he challenged and quirked an eyebrow. In the next moment he was running across the sand. Suzie couldn't help but shriek with laughter as she chased after him. She hadn't felt more like a little kid in years. She lengthened her strides, determined to tackle Paul and make him pay.

They had been out on the water most of the day. Paul was determined to get her alone as often as he could now. Suzie had made arrangements with Mary to keep an eye on Dune House, her stunning bed and breakfast, while she was gone. But she still felt a little guilty for having so much fun, when she was sure that Mary was back home toiling away with bed linens and dust rags.

One thing she did not feel guilty about was dumping an entire bucket of cold water all over the top of Paul's head.

"Hey!" he complained and groaned at the same time. "It's not fair, I don't have much cover up there!"

She laughed at his reference to the fact that his thick, brown hair was gradually retreating along his scalp. She thought it added to his burly look, which she found to be incredibly attractive.

"It's fair play," Suzie teased him as she backed away from him giggling. Her own skirt was soaked through because he had decided to douse her with water a few minutes before. As they were enjoying the beach, they were surrounded only by nature. One of the best parts about going out on the boat with Paul was that he knew all of the hidden hideaways. This beach in particular looked as if it hadn't seen a human footprint in years.

"That's it," he said gruffly as he locked eyes with her. "This is war."

"War?" Suzie gulped and started to run. Despite the fact that Paul was a rather brawny man, he was very light on his feet. He managed to catch up to her in three bouncing strides. When she felt his strong arms collide with her waist, a sharp thrill raced through her. He was careful to hold her close to keep her from crashing into the sand.

"Now, what will I do with you?" he whispered, his breath lingering close to her ear. Suzie had a few ideas. But before she could volunteer them, they both heard a strange sound that startled them out of their romantic trance.

"What was that?" Suzie wondered as she looked in the direction of the sound. It was similar to a woman crying, but it had just enough of a trill to it that it was clear it was an animal, not a person.

"Oh, that would be Bonnie Blue," he said with a sigh. "She must be jealous."

"Bonnie Blue?" Suzie asked as she unwound reluctantly from his arms. "Is that a friend of yours?"

"You could say that," Paul smiled as he slipped his hand in hers. "We've known each other a long time."

"Oh?" Suzie felt a little confused. She was beginning to wonder if Paul was talking about a real woman.

"You see, before I had the good luck of meeting you, I spent a lot of time alone," he smiled as he led her towards a gathering of trees further down the beach. "In fact, I spent a lot of time here. It was a quiet place that I could anchor the boat and camp if I wanted. I just loved the fact that most people had no idea where I was."

"I can understand that," Suzie said with a slight nod. She had lived an adventurous life as an investigative reporter and there had been more than a few times when she wished she could just disappear. She smiled fondly at him as they stepped through the trees. It meant a lot to her that he would share his secret retreat with her.

"When I stayed here though, I wasn't alone. This crane became a part of my life. I tried to shoo her away, but she was quite insistent," he laughed a little. "Eventually I just became accustomed to her greeting me and hovering over me when I visited. I named her Bonnie Blue, because her feathers look almost blue in the right light," he explained.

"A crane?" Suzie grinned. She had started to get jealous over a bird. Then she caught sight of Bonnie Blue. The bird was quite regal as she perched on the precipice of a large rock that jutted up out of the water. The beach that surrounded

Bonnie Blue was a beautiful one, with flawless, white sand. But what made it unique was the foliage that grew right up to its edge. There must have been enough fertile soil to support the bushes, flowers, and tall grass that stretched towards the sunny sky. It was truly one of the most stunning places that Suzie had ever observed. Bonnie Blue turned to look at Suzie. She released another mournful cry.

"She likes you," Paul said with pride.

"Oh, good," Suzie laughed. "I'd hate to see what she would do if she didn't like me."

"I like you," Paul said and gazed into her eyes lovingly. Their relationship was still fresh. They had only shared a few kisses, but they had been amazing. Suzie was still hesitant, she hadn't set out on this part of her life with the intention of finding romance, but Paul was more than just romance. He felt like the perfect fit for her. When he studied her so intently, preparing to kiss her, her heart sped up and she felt giddy. When he kissed her, Bonnie Blue let out a shrill cry and flew off across the sea.

"Hmm, she is jealous," Paul laughed as he broke the kiss.

"Well, she's going to have to come to terms with another woman being in your life," she said in a serious tone.

"I'm sure she'll come around," Paul murmured and stole another kiss. When Suzie pulled away and rested her head against his shoulder, he held her comfortably against him. She felt as if the day could not have been more perfect. She was quite far from the condo she had holed herself up in not long ago, and she had Dune House and her best friend Mary to thank for all of it.

Paul spread out a blanket on the sand and settled a picnic basket down in the middle of it. Suzie had packed it for their trip. As she began spreading out the food, Paul was busy sifting his fingers through the sand.

"Aren't you hungry?" Suzie asked as she looked over at him.

"Just a minute," he nodded. "I'm looking for something. Aha, here it is," he added as he pulled a seashell out of the sand. It was perfectly rounded and rose shaded.

"It's beautiful," Suzie said as she studied it intently.

"This beach is the only place I've ever found one like this," Paul admitted. "It's for you," he added as he handed it to her. "Might not be jewelry, but maybe you could turn it into a necklace or something," he added shyly. Suzie had noticed the only thing that Paul seemed to be insecure about was his income. He lived by the sea, and if the sea wasn't in a generous mood, he didn't always make a lot. He had made a few comments about not being able to buy her the things he wanted to.

8

"It's priceless," she replied honestly. She smiled and tucked it into her pocket. "But if I'm going to have one, then you have to have one, too," she sifted through the sand until she found another slightly smaller shell.

"Here you go," she smiled as she handed it to him. "Now we have a matching pair."

"Wonderful," he murmured as he looked into her eyes. He tucked the shell into his pocket and then shifted a little closer to her on the blanket. "Now, about being hungry," he growled and moved to kiss her. Suzie stuck a roll between his lips before he could get too close.

"Good because I made plenty," she laughed as he sputtered on the roll and then shook his head.

"Let's eat," he said with a good natured smile and they shared their picnic, tossing a few crumbs here and there to Bonnie Blue who was standing guard.

The boat ride back to Dune House was

smooth. Suzie leaned close to Paul as he steered the boat. She noticed he always stood tall at the helm, never a slouched shoulder in sight. She was sure that he was living his true passion. It was something that she admired about him, and something she was learning to do herself. Despite many years as an investigative reporter her real passion had always been design, interior decorating in particular. Converting the home she had inherited from her late Uncle Harry back into a bed and breakfast had given her that opportunity.

"Too bad the sun has to set," Paul said softly as he steered the boat into the marina.

"Would you like to come over for some wine?" Suzie offered once the boat had been docked.

"Not tonight," he said with a slight shake of his head. "I have to meet with someone in the morning, and I want my mind to be clear."

Suzie raised an eyebrow as she wondered who

he was meeting. She paused a moment, to see if he would tell her. But Paul was already stepping onto the dock and reaching back to help her across. He tended to keep most things to himself, not in a closed off way, but in the way of someone who was in the habit of being alone.

Paul walked her back to Dune House. When they reached the end of the long drive, he pulled her into his arms.

"One last kiss?" he pleaded as he held her close. Paul was strong, and Suzie loved the way his body seemed to engulf her slighter form.

"Just one?" she pouted with playful disappointment.

He kissed her before she could say another word. Then again. Then once more, until she pushed him away with a laugh.

"All right, remember your meeting in the morning," she winked at him. He watched as she walked towards Dune House and then he turned and walked back off towards the marina.

***

When Suzie stepped through the front door she heard Mary on the phone. It sounded like she was setting up a guest for a few days later in the week. Suzie hung out by the front desk until Mary hung up the phone.

"New guests?" she asked with a smile.

"Yes, nothing too wild, just a couple that wants a night away," Mary smiled. "Sounds like it might be their first time leaving the baby behind."

"We'll make sure they have some privacy then," Suzie said fondly.

"So, spill," Mary said as she walked around the front desk. "How was your romantic getaway with Paul?"

"Quite romantic," Suzie admitted with a

teasing smile. "He really is an amazing man."

"Well, that makes sense, since you're an amazing woman," Mary pointed out. "But no details?"

"I'm afraid not," Suzie grinned shyly. "What happens on the boat stays on the boat."

Mary offered a dramatic sigh. "Well, I guess I will just have to muddle through my boring life then."

"I don't think you've ever been boring, Mary," Suzie said warmly.

"I do like to keep things lively," Mary winked lightly and then yawned. "I am worn out tonight though. I did some of the vacuuming upstairs. Would you mind finishing down here?"

"Not at all," Suzie said quickly. "And I'll wash off the deck chairs, too. I'm nowhere near ready for bed."

"Ah, to be young and in love," Mary rolled her eyes.

"Young?" Suzie quirked a brow. "You know that we're about the same age, Mary."

"Yes," Mary agreed. "But love makes you young."

Suzie had to smile at that. She recalled the way she had been chasing Paul around the beach. She had felt young then. Not that she ever really felt old, she didn't think she would be old until she hit her nineties, and even then it would be debatable. But she hadn't felt so young until she met Paul.

"Good night, Mary," Suzie said. "I'll vacuum first so that you can get some sleep."

Mary blew a kiss over her shoulder and headed up the stairs to her room. Suzie pulled the vacuum cleaner from the bottom of the stairs and started in the hallway that led to the game room. As she was vacuuming her mind drifted over her day. She already missed Paul. Occasionally she thought about what it would be like to wake up next to him, or at least have the luxury of sharing breakfast with him each morning. But it was a thought that was always chased away by her independent streak. She had plenty of lovers in her time, but none of them were what she would label as commitments. They were fun, they were hot, but they were not meant to be permanent. It felt so very different with Paul, as if maybe, it was meant to be.

Shaking the thought from her mind she finished the vacuuming and put the vacuum away in the storage closet. Then she headed out to the deck to spray off the deck chairs. She could hear the water rushing against the sand. Everything else was quiet. Garber was a town that rarely ever stayed up late. Even during the weekend most party-goers were silent and home well before midnight. As she sprayed off the deck chairs she smiled at the sight of Dune House towering above her. It had changed a lot on the inside, but as for the outside not much had been done. The old sprawling house was filled with character and she wanted it to remain that way. It was a draw for those seeking a romantic spot that was quite different from the usual run of the mill hotel.

She rolled the hose up and put it away. Then she pushed the deck chairs to the edge of the deck so that they would get the full sun in the morning. The ocean caught her eye as its waves rolled silver in the moonlight. The shade reminded her every time of Paul's eyes, as if the ocean had found its way inside him, and made him part of it.

"All right, Suzie, you're getting out of control with this mushy stuff," she admonished herself as she walked back towards the front door of Dune House. She still couldn't help stealing a glance towards the marina where several boats, including Paul's were docked. She wondered if he was looking out in the direction of Dune House at the same time.

Chapter Two

The next morning Suzie woke up early. Sometimes she felt like she was in a race with Mary to do her share of the work. Mary was accustomed to taking care of others, and a house. But Dune House was much larger than anything she had ever lived in, and Suzie hated to see her taking on more of the workload. She got up, determined to take care of the runners in the front hall before Mary had the chance to. She rolled up the rug and carried it out onto the front porch. She was beating the dirt and dust from it when she heard someone call out to her.

"Morning, beautiful," Paul said as he walked down the driveway. Even though it was just past seven, Suzie was sure he had already been up for quite some time. He was an early riser. He was also not alone. There was a young man scuffing along beside him, his hands sunk deep into his pockets. He had a baseball cap pulled down low over his forehead.

"Hi Paul," Suzie smiled warmly as Paul ascended the steps onto the wraparound porch.

"Hi Suzie," he replied with an equally warm expression. "I was wondering if you could do me a favor?"

"Of course, what is it?" Suzie asked as she looked from Paul to the man he had walked up with. From what she could see of him, she was sure he was quite young, barely in his twenties, if that. He adjusted the hat on his head which cast more shadow across his face and his eyes flitted nervously around. Suzie felt a little uneasy about him right away.

"This is Trent, he's a new deckhand that I just hired for a fishing trip. He needs a place to stay, so I was wondering if you could rent him a room for the night?" Paul glanced over at Trent. "Trent, this is my girlfriend Suzie."

Suzie's heart stopped for a moment at his description. She hadn't heard him call her that yet. She decided that she kind of liked it.

"Nice to meet you, Trent," she said and smiled at the young man. He looked at her with pale blue eyes. They were a beautiful shade, but something about them seemed to be shifty.

"You too, Miss," he replied calmly. Suzie tilted her head slightly to the side as she studied Trent. He seemed polite enough.

"Well, we have plenty of rooms available," Suzie said as she realized that Paul was still waiting for an answer. "Let me show you one, Trent," she invited. As she stepped into Dune House, Trent and Paul filed in behind her.

"Nice place," Trent commented. It was clear that Trent was a man of few words.

"It's one of the oldest houses in the entire town of Garber," Paul gushed with pride. "Suzie and her friend Mary have worked very hard restoring it."

"With plenty of help from you, Paul," she reminded him with warmth in her voice.

"Great," Trent nodded.

"I just need to enter your details in the computer," Suzie said as she walked towards the computer.

"Sure," he said as she typed in the information that he rattled off.

"Okay, let me show you a room," Suzie said as she walked towards one of the available rooms.

"You can stay here, Trent, there are extra blankets and pillows in the closet. You're welcome to have breakfast with us in the morning," Suzie smiled.

"No thanks, I keep to myself," Trent said. Then he nodded at Paul and stepped into the room. Suzie was a little surprised when he closed the door behind him. Paul grimaced and walked back with her towards the living room.

"He's not the friendliest soul," he said with a shake of his head. "To be honest I'm taking a chance on him, because he hasn't been a deckhand long. But I need some help on this next run, and he's available, so off we go."

"Are you sure about him?" Suzie asked hesitantly. "He just seems a little off."

"Most men who spend their time on a boat are," Paul laughed. "You've just become used to it with me."

"You may be right about that," she grinned. "Well, he's welcome to stay."

"Thanks," Paul nodded as Suzie walked over to the front desk.

"So, this is a big job?" she asked with a slight frown.

"Yes, but it's a quick one," he shrugged. "At least it will be with an extra set of hands. I wanted to try to be free for the weekend," he added. "In case you let me whisk you away."

"Paul, that sounds great," Suzie said. "But I do have some guests coming in over the weekend. You know that tends to be our busiest time."

"I know, so I can be here to help if you need it, or just to rub your feet," he suggested.

"Oh a foot rub does sound nice," Suzie giggled. "But you're the one who will be working hard. Just promise me that you'll be safe."

"I always am," he replied.

"Promise?" Suzie insisted as she looked into his eyes.

"Promise," he replied before offering her a light kiss. "I have to run some errands for the trip."

"Have fun," Suzie grinned.

"You already did the runners didn't you?" Mary asked from the top of the stairs with a huff.

"Beat you to it!" Suzie declared. "I just have to pull them in."

"Not if I get to them first," Mary said as she hurried down the stairs. The rest of the day was an all-out race to see who would get the cleaning and preparation tasks done first. Suzie never noticed Trent coming or going from his room. She assumed he might be sleeping in preparation for his journey, but she still couldn't shake the way she felt. At dinner when she knocked on his door to see if he wanted to join them, all she received was a gruff 'No'.

Suzie was glad to be able to do a favor for Paul, but something about Trent just left her uneasy.

"Make sure that you lock your door tonight," she murmured to Mary as they walked down the hall to go to bed.

"I always do," Mary said. "Why? Is there something you're uncomfortable about?"

"I just don't know if I trust Trent," Suzie replied hesitantly. "It just seems like there is something off about him."

"I understand," Mary nodded. "You have to trust your instincts, Suzie."

"Thanks, Mary," she smiled. "At least he will only be around for a few days."

"Yes and most of that he will be on the boat with Paul," Mary reminded her. "But if you feel uncomfortable about anything, please tell me?" she smiled warmly at her friend.

"Yes, I will," Suzie replied and gave Mary a hug goodnight. As Suzie stepped into her room she glanced around at its contents. She loved decorating so her room had the most flare of all the rooms in Dune House. She changed her style often. The latest motif was black and white with French Quarter influences. It exuded a sense of romance and mystery, which was exactly how she felt about her relationship with Paul at the moment. She knew that he wanted more, but she was dragging her feet.

For so long her life had solely been about her.

She had watched Mary engage herself to one man, dedicate her life to one man, and witnessed the hurt that her friend experienced when that man only returned her love with hurt. Of course there had been the rare occasion that Suzie felt some envy of the married life. But it was a fleeting feeling, and was easily swept away by tearful conversations with Mary. She never wanted anything to dampen her freedom, or hold back her creativity.

But that's not how she felt with Paul. If anything she felt freer than she ever had. He inspired her creativity so much that she had painted her feelings for him all over her walls. As she sprawled out across her bed, she thought of him for the thousandth time. She closed her eyes and remembered their latest excursion on the beach, and how lovely it had been to share that special memory with only him.

Chapter Three

The next morning Suzie woke up to the aroma of French toast and coffee. She smiled to herself. They didn't often have guests during the week so Mary was outdoing herself to persuade Trent to have a hot breakfast. Suzie doubted that he would even get up for breakfast as he had mentioned the day before that he didn't want it. She didn't want Mary to be disappointed, plus the food smelled delicious.

Suzie dressed quickly. She caught a glimpse of her brassy blond hair in the mirror and cringed. She had been so busy with Dune House and Paul that she hadn't kept up with dying it. It needed a few touch ups. She ran her fingers across the faint discoloration under her bright blue eyes. Mary insisted that no one else could see it, but Suzie was feeling more and more self-conscious about it. With a sigh she headed out into the hallway and down the stairs to join Mary for breakfast.

As she stepped out into the dining room area, she spotted Trent sitting at the table. But there was also someone else sitting beside him. Paul in his usual dark blue top and faded jeans. He always looked so relaxed in his work clothes. Suzie studied him for a few minutes while he didn't know that she was there. She loved the way his eyes crinkled when he smiled, lightening the brooding gray color. She adored the subtle twitch of his upper lip when he was trying to hold back a laugh. He was telling Trent a story about one of his fishing trips.

"So, I tried to reel this huge sucker in," he explained. "But it was fighting me tooth and nail. It kept flipping and twirling in the water. By the time I got him out, he was wound up tight like a spool of thread. I was so excited that I had won the battle, I didn't even pay attention to what I was doing. I just cut the fishing line. Next thing I know it unraveled and that fish plopped right back in the water and swam away."

"Huh," Trent narrowed his eyes. "Shouldn't have cut the line until he was in the bin."

"I know that," Paul said impatiently. "That's the point of the story. The battle isn't won until it's won."

"Right," Trent cleared his throat and stabbed his fork into a portion of his French toast.

"I think it's a lovely story," Suzie said as she stepped up behind Paul.

"Suzie," he smiled warmly and stood up from his chair to greet her. Suzie hesitated just a little. Trent was their guest, and she was officially on duty. But she couldn't resist the soft kiss that Paul offered.

"I hope you don't mind," Paul said quickly. "Mary extended the invite, since we're launching right after breakfast today."

"Oh, I'm sure she doesn't mind," Mary called teasingly from the kitchen.

"I don't mind at all," Suzie replied happily. "Will you two be gone long?" she asked.

"Just two days," Paul replied. "Going to get Trent's feet wet," he grinned.

Trent seemed oblivious to Paul's remarks. Suzie tried to keep a smile on her face. She had no idea how Paul was going to tolerate being stuck on a boat with Trent for two days. She could barely stand him for more than a few minutes. This was quite odd for her, because she usually could handle any personality thrown at her. In her line of work as a reporter she had to be able to communicate with all kinds of people. She didn't always like everyone she met, but she could deal with them. However, Trent was a different story.

"More French toast?" Mary offered as she stepped into the dining room.

"No, coffee," Trent replied without looking up. Suzie noticed Paul's jaw clench. He wasn't always the most amiable person, but he had strict, old fashioned standards about how women should be treated.

"I'd love some, Mary, thank you," Paul said with a smile, though his eyes were still locked on Trent.

"Wonderful," Mary said and slid two more slices of French toast onto his plate.

"I'll get the coffee," Suzie said with an edge in her voice. "Would you like some as well, Paul?" she asked.

"Yes please, I could use a fresh cup," Paul replied smoothly. "Thank you very much."

Suzie followed Mary back into the kitchen.

"How did you not toss that plate of French toast into Trent's lap?" she asked while she walked over to the coffee pot.

"Now, Suzie, we have to make customer service a top priority," Mary laughed.

"Seriously though, how do you have so much

patience?" Suzie demanded. "I need to borrow some!"

"Well, the toddler years, and the teenage years," Mary laughed. "My kids taught me a lot about how to tolerate some very bad attitudes."

"You are my attitude guru," Suzie said and bowed playfully before pouring four cups of coffee. She placed the coffee on a silver tray along with some cream, sugar, and stirrers.

"Patience can be learned in a lot of ways," Mary reminded her. "I wish I had as much confidence and determination as you do. That's something no one has ever taught me."

"There's still plenty of time," Suzie replied warmly as she walked out into the dining area carefully carrying the tray. As she was about to set it down on the table, her foot caught on one of the chair legs. The tray tilted as her balance wavered. She managed to keep the coffee cups on the tray, but the cold container of cream slipped right off the lip of the tray and onto Trent's lap.

"Ah!" Trent screamed as he jumped up from his chair. "What's wrong with you?" he demanded as he glared at her. "You clumsy cow, you could have burned me with that coffee. What kind of place is this?" he demanded.

Before he could say another word, Paul had him pinned against the wall with one hand wrapped loosely around his throat. Trent was clawing at Paul's wrist, but Paul didn't even seem to notice Trent's nails digging deep into his skin.

"Don't you ever speak to her that way," he growled.

Suzie was so flustered by her mistake that she couldn't even comprehend what was happening between Paul and Trent. In the same moment Suzie's cousin, Jason, and one of his fellow police officers stepped into the dining room.

"Hey, what's happening here?" Jason demanded sharply as he glared at the two men.

"Paul, let go of him, now."

Trent was struggling to get free. Mary ran in from the kitchen to see what all of the commotion was about.

"Suzie, what's happened?" she asked swiftly.

"I'm so sorry," Suzie said quickly. "It's all my fault, I slipped and the tray..."

"No," Paul barked. He had ignored Jason's command. Both Jason and his partner were getting more demanding as they commanded Paul to let go of Trent. "This boy needs to learn some manners. She made a mistake, Trent, it happens. It doesn't give you the right to speak in such a vile way. Do you have something to say?" he asked as if he was correcting a young child.

"Sorry," Trent croaked out, his eyes wide.

"Paul, enough!" Jason demanded as he stepped closer to the pair. "Let go of him now or I'll have you in handcuffs."

Suzie's heart was racing. What had started out

as a lovely morning had quickly become something terrible.

"It's okay, Paul, please, let him go," she murmured, flushed with embarrassment.

Paul reluctantly let go of Trent.

"I'm sorry," Trent muttered again. "It just surprised me."

"I understand," Suzie replied, though she didn't completely. She had seen a look of hatred in Trent's eyes that made her very nervous.

"I don't," Paul warned. "You better rein in that attitude or you can forget about the job I offered you," he warned.

"Here, let me clean it up," Trent offered and took the towel from Mary's hand. He began mopping up the cream that was spilled on the floor. His entire demeanor appeared to have changed. But Suzie could still see the anger in his sharp gestures.

"See, everything is settled," Paul said

brusquely as he looked over at Jason.

"Unless he decides to press charges for assault," Jason pointed out with clear annoyance. "Paul, I could arrest you for ignoring my instructions."

Paul locked eyes with Jason. He didn't have to say a word, his expression said it for him.

"Aw Jason, everything seems settled now," his partner said mildly.

"Are you okay, Suzie?" Jason asked as he turned to her. "Mary?" he asked.

"I'm fine," Suzie replied, still a little shaken. Mary nodded and picked up the container of cream.

"I just wanted to stop by and say hello, introduce you to my new partner," Jason explained calmly, though his eyes kept drifting back towards Paul with a hint of animosity. "This is Kirk Rondella."

Kirk tipped his hat slightly. He looked about

ten years Jason's senior. His hair was shaved close to his scalp. His stance reminded Suzie of some of the military men she had done interviews with.

"Nice to meet you, Kirk," Suzie said and managed a smile. "Welcome to Dune House. I'm sorry for the chaos," she frowned. "Just one of those crazy mornings."

"Seems that way," Jason said, his voice still edgy.

"Trent is my new deckhand," Paul explained courteously.

Jason only nodded slightly. It was clear that he was still rankled by Paul's behavior.

"Let me get us all some fresh cream, and Jason, Kirk would you like some coffee?" Suzie offered.

"There's plenty of French toast," Mary suggested warmly.

Jason glanced over at Kirk, who was grinning from ear to ear.

"We have a few minutes before patrol starts," Jason agreed. "Thank you."

Suzie and Mary slipped back into the kitchen while the four men settled around the table.

"What was that about?" Mary demanded as soon as they were alone in the kitchen.

"I spilled the cream in Trent's lap," Suzie admitted, still mortified. "He said some rude things to me, and Paul jumped into action. It was a little over the top, don't you think?" she asked hesitantly.

"Paul was just coming to your defense," Mary pointed out. "You were right about Trent's attitude. Maybe some time alone on the boat with Paul will teach him some proper manners."

"Maybe," Suzie frowned as she poured two more cups of coffee. "But I hope that it doesn't end up with one of them tossed overboard."

"At least you know it won't be Paul," Mary smiled confidently as she prepared a plate filled with slices of French toast.

"I still think it was a little over the top," Suzie shook her head.

"Suzie," Mary said as she picked up the plate. "You have to admit, it must have felt wonderful to have a man come to your defense that way."

"Maybe just a little," Suzie replied as she tried to hide her smile.

"Paul is still nervous," Mary added. "So, he went a little overboard, it didn't seem like Trent minded."

"I know, but I can fight my own battles," Suzie pointed out. She carried the two cups of coffee instead of placing them on a tray. Mary picked up the fresh cream.

"Yes, of course you can," Mary agreed with a soft sigh. "But it is nice when you don't always have to fight them on your own."

Suzie smiled sympathetically. She knew that Mary had often had to battle through things on her own.

"Maybe I'm being a little too sensitive," she agreed. But she still felt very unsettled. Trent's presence had her on edge, but Paul's behavior had made her even more confused. As they walked back into the dining room they were greeted by uproarious laughter from the group of men. It seemed as if the disturbance from a few moments before had been forgotten. Suzie and Mary sat down at the table with the others, and joined into the conversation.

"It isn't easy being a rookie," Jason said, red-faced. "How was I supposed to know that he was a mime?"

"The not talking didn't give you a hint?" Kirk joked lightly.

"It seemed like non-compliance to me," Jason chuckled.

Suzie smiled at her young cousin. She knew he tried hard to be the best police officer he could be.

"Did you restrain him in an invisible box?" she asked, drawing more laughter from the group.

"Let's just say that he had a little difficulty once the handcuffs were on," Jason laughed.

"Well, luckily for me I have a seasoned officer to protect me from those pitfalls," Kirk volunteered with a grin.

"It's always good to have someone experienced to learn from," Paul agreed and cast a short glance in Trent's direction.

"True," Trent offered, though he was busy preparing his coffee. He still seemed detached from the rest of the conversation.

Jason and Kirk polished off their coffee and breakfast quickly.

"Time to be on the lookout for those dangerous mimes," Kirk quipped as he stood up from his chair.

"Ha ha," Jason retorted with a grin.

"It was a pleasure to meet you, Kirk," Suzie said. "I'm sure we'll be seeing plenty more of you."

"I hope so," Kirk said. "That French toast was delicious. Thank you, both."

"Anytime," Mary smiled.

As Jason and Kirk left, Paul locked eyes with Suzie. "Do you have a moment before we set sail?" he asked.

"Of course," Suzie nodded.

"I'll just take these to the kitchen," Mary said as she began clearing the plates. Amazingly Trent stood up and began gathering the coffee cups. Once the two had disappeared into the kitchen, Paul walked over to Suzie's chair.

"I'm sorry if I was a little out of bounds," he said swiftly. "I just couldn't stand him talking to you that way."

"I understand," Suzie smiled. "But you can't

do that to all of our unruly patrons."

"I know," he agreed. "Trent just has a way of pushing my buttons. I hope the trip goes smoothly."

Suzie was a little surprised by his comment. She wondered if he felt the same uneasiness about Trent that she did.

"Just be careful, okay?" she asked as she looked into his eyes.

"Always," he replied and kissed her gently. "I'll be back soon," he promised.

After Trent and Paul left, Suzie walked back into the kitchen to wash the dishes.

"Looks like Paul really knocked some sense into Trent," Mary commented as she helped clean up.

"I hope so," Suzie said reluctantly. "I don't think they're a good match to work together."

"Two days trapped on a boat should cure

that," Mary laughed lightly.

Chapter Four

With Trent gone there wasn't much to do at Dune House. Suzie occupied herself with catching up on a novel she had been meaning to read. Mary was busy talking with her daughter on the telephone about the new semester of college classes she was lining up. As Suzie tried to concentrate on her book, her mind kept drifting back to Paul, and to Trent. She was a little more worried than usual about Paul being out on the water. By the evening she became a little more relaxed. She found Mary sitting out on the section of porch that overlooked the water. The sun was just beginning to set.

"Did you have a nice chat?" she asked as she sat down beside Mary.

"Oh yes," Mary said happily. "She's really passionate about school this year."

"I'm glad," Suzie smiled. She knew that Mary

worried about her children, but both seemed to be off to a fantastic start as adults. "Would you like to take a walk?" Suzie offered.

"Yes, need to work out these knees," Mary agreed as she stood up. Mary's knees gave her some trouble from time to time, she called it getting older, Suzie called it having too much weight on her shoulders for too many years. As they stepped down into the sand Suzie sighed contentedly. She was really starting to settle into life at Dune House and the quaint beachside town of Garber.

"I wonder how far out they are?" she muttered casually as she looked out over the water.

"Isn't it strange to think there are so many people out on the water while we're walking on the sand?" Mary mused. "Sometimes the ocean seems like an eternity."

"It sure does," Suzie agreed with a touch of worry.

"Are you still concerned about Paul and Trent getting along?" Mary asked.

"A little," Suzie admitted.

"Men have a different way of getting along," Mary said softly. "I can't say I understand it."

"I'm not sure I would care to," Suzie laughed, but her laughter faded as she heard sirens wailing in the distance.

"What do you think is going on?" Mary asked when she saw a police boat zip across the water. It was from the next town over, with Parish clearly marked on the side of the boat.

"I don't know," Suzie said with a frown. "But at least it's not happening in Garber."

They had walked almost a mile along the beach when they finally turned back. The sun was disappearing and the sky was becoming littered with stars.

"I couldn't imagine a better way to spend an evening," Mary said as she kept pace with Suzie.

"Do you ever miss the adventure of your old career?" she asked.

"Probably about as much as you miss the adventure of the teenage years," Suzie grinned. When they reached Dune House again, Jason was waiting for them on the porch. His partner was not with him.

"Hi Jason," Suzie said cheerfully, but her jovial attitude faded when she saw his grim expression.

"Is something wrong?" Mary asked.

"I don't know how to tell you this, Suzie, but there's been an incident," he cleared his throat.

"Is that what the police boat was about?" she asked.

"Yes, it's not my jurisdiction, but I wanted to tell you myself," he frowned and gestured to one of the benches on the porch. "Maybe you should sit down."

"It's not Paul is it?" Suzie gasped. "If it is, just

tell me, Jason!"

"It's not Paul exactly," Jason said. "Trent's body was found in Parish, it looks like it was washed ashore."

"What?" Mary muttered in shock. "His body? Do you mean that he is dead?"

Suzie was so stunned that she couldn't bring herself to speak. She finally forced some words past her lips. "Did the boat sink?" she asked.

"The coast guard has no reports of a boat in trouble," Jason explained. "All we know right now is that Trent's body was found on shore. He didn't drown, Suzie," he drew a shaky breath. "He was beat up pretty bad, and I heard that he might have been stabbed."

Suzie sat down on the bench as her legs began to give way. Mary wrapped her arm around her shoulders.

"Try not to worry too much, Suzie. I'm sure that there has to be an explanation. Paul will be here soon to tell us," she added.

"Look Suzie, I know that you and Paul have been dating, and so do the Parish police," he frowned.

"What? How do they know that?" she asked, still very confused.

"Because I told them," Jason admitted. "When they found out I knew Paul, they asked me some questions."

"Oh?" Suzie could barely focus on Jason. "Are they searching for the boat? What if Paul is in the water?"

"Suzie, all of Parish's police force is on this. A few of the locals are looking into it, too, but we really can't investigate it," he hesitated a moment and then looked directly into her eyes. "The tracking system has been disabled on Paul's boat and I think they consider him a suspect at the moment. They may want to question you about his relationship to Trent."

49

"Why would they think that?" she demanded with frustration. "If Trent is dead, Paul must be hurt or overboard. He wouldn't have let anything happen to Trent."

"That's not how it looked this morning," Jason said uneasily.

"Jason," Suzie stared hard at him. "Did you tell the Parish police about the argument this morning?"

"It was more than an argument," Jason said defensively. "You have to understand, Suzie, I'm an officer of the law, I can't just hide information that could be important in a murder case."

"You are insane if you think that Paul had anything to do with Trent's death," Suzie shot back. Suddenly her legs had strength again. She stood up and glared directly at Jason. "You know he didn't do this."

"I didn't say I suspected him," Jason said as he raised his hands in innocence. "But with Kirk at my side, I had to demonstrate proper protocol, I had to inform the Parish police officer about what I had seen. How could I explain it if I didn't?"

"Unbelievable," Suzie said with fury in her voice.

"Suzie," Mary said gently as she took her friend's arm in her own. "Jason has a point. He was just doing his job. But all three of us know that Paul wouldn't have done this. Like you said, I'm sure that Paul will be here soon to clear all of this up."

"Let's hope so," Jason frowned. "I know that you're upset with me, Suzie, but I had no other choice."

Suzie frowned and shook her head. She knew that Jason had to tell the truth to the other officer, but it made her sick to her stomach to think that Paul was being treated as a suspect.

"What if they don't find him?" she moaned.

"What if he's out there somewhere suffering and no one finds him?"

"I'm sorry, Suzie," Jason murmured.

"It's going to be okay," Mary said firmly. "It has to be okay. We all just need to process this. Jason, is there any way you can get on the investigation?" she asked hopefully.

"I can't," Jason shook his head. "Parish has a much larger police department and they are very territorial. The captain already told me directly to stay out of it. I argued with him which he wasn't very impressed about but I managed to convince him to let me be the one to tell you what had happened as I said that if I told you then I might be able find out if you knew anything about Paul's location. But he made me promise to stay out of it once I had spoken to you."

Suzie's expression softened at his words. She knew how important being a police officer was to Jason, yet he was willing to argue with his superior so he could be the one to break the news to her straight away.

"Thank you, Jason," she whispered. "I just can't believe this is happening. Can you take me to where Trent was found?"

"It's not a good idea tonight, Suzie," Jason said firmly. "The police are doing a full investigation, you won't be able to get anywhere near there. All we can do tonight is hope that Paul shows up with an explanation."

"I have to do more than that," Suzie said with determination.

"I'm warning you, Suzie, if you get in the middle of their investigation, they will not be happy. Parish PD is not like Garber, they will not hesitate to make you face consequences for interfering. I really should get going I'm in the middle of my shift," he frowned. "Are you going to be okay, Suzie?"

"No," Suzie replied with wide eyes. "No, I

won't be okay until Paul is standing here beside me, safe and sound."

"It's okay, Jason, I'll be with her," Mary assured him. "But please call us if you hear anything more."

"Of course," he nodded and took one long look at Suzie. "I'm sorry, Suzie."

Suzie could only nod before turning to look out over the vast ocean. "Where are you, Paul?" she whispered.

Chapter Five

"This can't be happening," Suzie kept repeating as she paced back and forth across the living room. Mary was perched on the edge of the couch as if she was prepared to tackle Suzie if she bolted for the door.

"It's going to be okay," Mary said for what might have been the hundredth time.

"How?" Suzie asked as she turned to face her friend. "How could this possibly be okay? Not only is Trent dead, but Paul is the main suspect in his death. You and I both know that Paul couldn't have killed him, so where does that leave Paul?" she gasped out.

"I...," Mary tried to think of something that would comfort Suzie, but no good solution came to her mind. "I'm sorry, Suzie, I'm just not sure," she finally replied before closing her eyes.

"I think there has to be something I can find

out at the crime scene," Suzie said firmly. "I need to be there, not holed up here waiting for news that may never come."

"You heard what Jason said, Suzie," Mary warned her sharply. "If we get in the middle of the investigation it might look even worse when it comes to their suspicion of Paul."

"Suspicion of Paul," Suzie blurted out with rage in her voice. "Those incompetent pinheaded cops from Parish couldn't run an investigation if they tripped and fell into the murderer."

"That's one person's opinion," a voice carried from the porch of Dune House. Suzie had left the door open in case Jason came back. She wasn't expecting anyone else. But the voice wasn't familiar. Suzie and Mary exchanged a quick nervous look before Suzie went walking towards the porch.

"Be careful, Suzie," Mary said as Suzie stepped through the open door and out onto the porch. Leaning against the front railing was a classic, small town police officer, right down to cowboy boots and a toothpick between his clenched teeth. Suzie noticed that like herself he appeared to be in his fifties, but that was where the similarity ended. His eyes were hard and icy as they settled on her.

"Are you Suzie Allen?" he asked.

"What if I am?" Suzie replied calmly and folded her arms across her stomach.

"Well, if you are Suzie Allen," the officer replied and paused to chew lightly on his toothpick. "Then you're who I need to talk to. My name is Officer Brown, and I work for Parish PD."

"Have you found Paul?" Suzie asked urgently. "Is he hurt?"

"So, you are Suzie Allen," he said as he narrowed his eyes once more. "Unfortunately, your boyfriend is still missing."

Suzie cringed at the term. It sounded so

juvenile when the officer said it.

"Are you looking for him?" Suzie gasped out. "He must be lost, or injured."

"Or he's on the run," the officer suggested in a hard voice. "He killed a man, and decided the best escape was to flee on his boat."

"He didn't kill anyone," Suzie argued with determination.

"Ma'am, are you going to deny that there was a physical confrontation over breakfast this morning?" he asked as he turned to face her. His muscular frame was rather intimidating. The way he flicked his toothpick was just as disturbing.

"There was a disagreement," she frowned. She knew that Jason had already told the police about it, so there was no point in lying.

"A disagreement that led to Paul's hands around Trent's throat," the officer clarified stiffly.

"One hand," Suzie huffed and lowered her eyes. "It was my fault. I spilled cream all over

Trent's pants, and Trent mouthed off about it, and well, Paul is very protective of me."

"Protective enough to kill someone?" he asked. "Maybe you even suggested it?"

Suzie stared at the officer with mounting dislike.

"I don't know what it is about your investigation that is leading you to such terrible conclusions, but I can assure you, Paul would never have anything to do with Trent's death. So, you are free to continue barking up the wrong tree, or you could actually do something to find a good man who is likely hurt or otherwise detained," she snapped sharply in return.

"Slow down there," he chuckled. "I'm not looking for a lecture. I'm here to ask you for a few answers, that's all. If you really want me to find your boyfriend, then you will answer me honestly."

"Fine," Suzie shook her head and braced

herself for the next questions.

"I want to know if there was anything between Paul and Trent. Had they met before Paul hired him?" he asked.

"No, I don't think so. Paul even said that Trent didn't have much experience, and that he was taking a chance on him," Suzie explained.

"Hmm, so he might have grown frustrated at Trent's lack of skill when it came to being a deckhand," the officer said and made a note.

"That is not what I said," Suzie said roughly. "You have a way of twisting things. Aren't you the least bit concerned about the truth in this situation? A man is dead, and his murderer is on the loose, while Paul is missing."

"Well, I'm very concerned," the officer replied and glared openly at her. "I'm concerned about finding the man who would kill a boy who was barely out of his teens, over what? Insulting his girlfriend?"

"If that makes sense to you then Parish PD is in a lot of trouble," Suzie said dismissively. "I don't have to answer any more questions. I want you off my property!"

"I see you have a bit of a temper as well," he said gravely and shook his head. "If I need any more information from you, I will be in contact. I expect you to cooperate with this investigation. Especially considering that you have law enforcement in your family."

"If you're referring to my cousin Officer Jason Allen, I think you should consult with him on what it's like to be a real police officer," Suzie snapped back. "Off my property," she demanded and pointed in the direction of the driveway. The officer shook his head. From the glint in his eyes Suzie suspected he might be trying to think of a reason to arrest her. Instead he just turned and walked down the steps. Mary inched her way out of the doorway of the house.

"Suzie, I can't believe you talked to him like

that," Mary said with awe in her voice. "Weren't you afraid that he would arrest you?"

"For what?" Suzie shrugged and sighed. "I might make my own citizen's arrest for impersonating a police officer since he doesn't have the ability to backup that badge."

"Wow, Suzie," Mary frowned. "You're on a bit of a roll. But you need to remember that Parish PD is in charge of this case. If they have more questions that same officer is likely to be the one that comes back."

"Well, I won't be here when he does," Suzie replied and stomped back into the house. "I'm not going to leave Paul out there, alone and hurt, while these idiots waste time trying to build a case against him."

"Suzie, promise me at least that you won't do anything until morning," Mary pleaded. "Then I will go with you to check out whatever you want to look into. If you try to go down there now you'll end up arrested, or worse. I know how upset you are, but you have to try to stay calm and think this through. You don't want to make things worse for Paul than they already are."

"It's okay, Mary," Suzie finally nodded. "You're right. I'm just going to try to get some rest, and so should you."

"Please Suzie, don't do anything rash," Mary warned her. "Or at least wake me up before you do."

"I promise," Suzie nodded solemnly. Once Mary headed off to her bedroom, Suzie walked towards her own room. She couldn't bring herself to close the door. It was like closing the reality of what was happening to Paul out of her mind. She walked over to the large windows that overlooked the water and pulled back the curtains. In the sky thunder rumbled low and long. She cringed at the sound. Would nature be so cruel as to toss a storm into the mix? If Paul was still out there somewhere on the water, in his boat or out, a storm could only complicate things.

"Please," Suzie whispered to the sky. "Keep him safe."

The words were muted by the fear in her voice. Even though she had promised Mary she would try to get some rest that was not a possibility. She pulled out her computer instead. She opened it up. It had been quite some time since she had drawn on her investigative skills, but she was going to need them. She searched Trent Baker. There were of course plenty of Trent Bakers in the world. She clicked on several of the results. But they all led to people that did not meet the description or age of the man she was looking for. She shifted gears and began searching Trent Baker associated with deckhand. There were still a few results, but they all led to dead ends. It was as if the Trent she had met did not exist.

Suzie knew that with Trent's young age he should have had his face and name splashed all over the internet from social media to blog posts.

But there was nothing on the internet that seemed to be directly related to him. Suzie was getting more frustrated by the moment. She slipped quietly out of her room and down the stairs to the front desk. She started the computer and pulled up Trent's information. She printed off the registration she had filled out for him. Then she took it back upstairs with her. She began searching his name associated with his birth date. Still she could not find a result that matched the Trent she knew.

In the technology age it was nearly impossible to keep yourself off the internet, so the deeper Suzie had to look the more suspicious she became. The only time she hadn't been able to find something on someone was when they were using an alias. Not many people set up social media under fake names because there was often no reason to. Maybe Trent Baker, wasn't Trent Baker at all. She glanced at her watch and waited impatiently for morning to come.

Chapter Six

Suzie waited until the sun finally rose above the sea. Then she pulled out her cell phone. She dialed Jason's number. He didn't answer. She dialed it again. On the third call he finally answered.

"Hello?" he mumbled half asleep.

"It's Suzie," she said quickly, guessing that his eyes were too blurry to even see her name on the caller ID.

"Suzie, what's wrong? Is it Paul?" he asked, his voice coming alive as he remembered what was happening.

"Nothing new," she said quickly. "But I'm going out to look at where Trent's body was found this morning. I just wanted you to know."

"Suzie, I really don't think you should," Jason said.

"There's no harm in going there, I won't touch anything," Suzie said. "But I have to do something, I can't sit here doing nothing."

"Okay, Suzie, if you do go there, make sure that you're careful. You don't need to paint a target on your back."

"I'll be careful," she promised him. "Jason, do you know if Parish PD had any trouble identifying Trent? I did some research on him last night, and I can't find a trace of him."

"I told you, Suzie, I'm not allowed to be involved. Parish PD is not telling me anything," he added gruffly, as if it was not for lack of trying. Suzie tried not to show her frustration. She knew it wasn't Jason's fault that he didn't have access to the investigation.

"Okay, I understand," she muttered.

"If there are still police where they found Trent, you need to stay back, understand?" he sighed before she could answer.

"Yes, of course, Jason," she replied.

"I should be going with you, Suzie, but if I'm spotted there it could be a big problem between Garber and Parish PD. Are you sure you're going to be okay?" he asked.

"I'll be fine," Suzie assured him before hanging up the phone. There was only one beach in Parish so she hoped it would just be a matter of walking along the beach until she found the crime scene tape. Suzie grabbed her purse. As she opened her door to the hallway, she found Mary waiting for her outside in the hall.

"I'm going with you," Mary said quickly.

"Are you sure, Mary?" Suzie asked hesitantly.

"No question," Mary replied. "I've got a few bagels for us ready to go."

"Thank you, Mary," Suzie said with relief. She was glad she would have company. She was a little afraid of what she might find at the scene.

"I'll drive," Mary offered.

Suzie was fine with that as she was sure that she would break a few laws if she was driving.

***

The city of Parish was much larger than Garber. It catered more to the business crowd, but still boasted a small strip of beach. The beach however was not a popular place to visit because of the crowded atmosphere of the town center. It was also not known to be a very friendly place. When Mary parked her car in a public beach access parking lot, Suzie looked for any police cars that might still be hovering. She didn't see any nearby. She knew Parish PD would not be far off, however.

Without hesitation Suzie climbed out of the car. Mary followed after her. As they walked across the beach looking for where the body was found, both women were silent. Suzie knew exactly what was on the line. She also knew that if Paul had any ability to communicate in any way he would have gotten a message to her to let her know that he was okay. Paul was most certainly not okay. He was also most certainly not a killer, at least in Suzie's mind.

"Looks like this is the place," Mary said quietly as they approached a section of the sand that was roped off by yellow police tape and wooden stakes.

If not for that barrier there would be no way to tell that any crime had taken place. The sand was so expansive, and so empty. There wasn't the slightest sign of a struggle. There were no footprints as the area was covered by water during high tide. The sand did not tell the story of what might have been Trent's last moments. From what Suzie knew, without evidence of what exactly had happened to Trent, the assumption had been made that he had been stabbed on Paul's boat and tossed out to sea, then he washed up on the shore. But Suzie knew that Paul's body could still be out there. Her entire body trembled at the thought. He might have been murdered right here. Suzie grasped the yellow tape that was blocking her way and began to duck under it.

"Suzie, maybe we shouldn't," Mary warned as she glanced nervously up and down the empty beach.

Suzie didn't reply. She continued to duck under the tape and stepped carefully into the sealed off patch of sand. She imagined Trent's body laying on the sand. If anything she would have wanted to be there just to see his position, any clues his body would have revealed. Of course, Trent's body had already been taken to the medical examiner's office. Suzie could barely restrain herself as she crouched down beside the sand. She wanted to see the truth in it. She wanted something to tell her that Paul was safe despite what all of her instincts were feeling.

"Suzie, are you okay?" Mary asked with a

frown as she stood beside her friend. "Try not to worry too much, we don't know for sure that Paul is even in danger."

"Mary, either Paul is in danger or he's a murderer, which do you think is more likely?" she asked incredulously as she looked up at her.

"I'm sorry," Mary mumbled. "I'm a little shocked, too."

"I know you are," Suzie said apologetically. "I know that you're only trying to help. I just can't believe that he's missing. There is nothing here, Mary," she breathed out. "Nothing but sand. Nothing to even give a hint as to where Paul or his boat might be."

As she spoke those words her cell phone began to chime. She reached into her pocket and pulled it out. Her eyes skimmed over the caller ID to see that it was Jason.

"Hey Jason," she said with a sigh. "There's nothing here."

"I know that," Jason replied quickly. "But that's not why I'm calling. I just spoke to my police chief and he confided that Paul's boat had been spotted further up the shore in Garber. I knew you would want to know. We had some men on it right away, but the boat is already gone. Suzie, this doesn't make things look better for Paul. There's chatter that he's looking for an easy escape route."

"Thank you for telling me, Jason," Suzie breathed a sigh of relief. Knowing that Paul's boat was still floating at least allowed her to believe that he hadn't gone down with it in the storm that had passed through the night before. It didn't provide an explanation as to his behavior, but it gave her slight peace of mind. "Can you tell me where it was spotted?"

"On Sunray Point," he replied. "About three miles north of Dune House. Don't be surprised if you get another visit from Parish PD. They might be expecting him to try to hide out at Dune House considering your relationship."

"Let them visit as much as they want," she replied sharply. "That officer couldn't solve a knock-knock joke."

"Just stay out of trouble, Suzie," Jason warned.

"I'll do my best," Suzie replied and hung up the phone. She looked over at Mary as she started walking back towards the car. "Paul's boat has been spotted about three miles north of Dune House, we need to get there as fast as possible."

"Did anyone see or talk to Paul?" Mary asked with urgency in her voice as she followed Suzie towards the parking lot.

"No, his boat was gone before they could, but I want to see where it was. Maybe he left something behind, or maybe there will be something to prove that he has been abducted or the boat has been stolen."

"At least it's almost good news," Mary sighed as she started the car.

Driving back into Garber was difficult. Suzie knew that she might never be able to share some of the special sights they passed with Paul again. She wanted to urge Mary to drive faster, but she was already going nearly twenty miles over the speed limit. Suzie spotted a Parish PD cruiser in the driveway of Dune House.

"Should we stop?" Mary asked.

"No," Suzie said firmly. "Keep going. If they want to waste their time thinking I know something about Paul's disappearance let them waste it alone."

They continued in the direction of Sunray point.

"Here it is, this is where Jason said Paul's boat

was spotted," Suzie said as she pointed to an old motel that was slumping along the beach. It was set for renovation but so far it was still an eyesore to most of the community. "Park over there," she suggested. The parking lot was empty. There was no sign of a police presence. Suzie and Mary locked the car and walked across the parking lot to the beach.

Again, this was an area of the beach that was mostly abandoned. Because of its location and the ample amount of pristine beach to enjoy, it was often ignored. Suzie found herself wondering who would even be out on this area of the beach to report seeing the boat. Flapping in the wind was more yellow police tape. It looked like the police had taken the sighting seriously enough to process the scene even though the boat was gone. Suzie walked over to the yellow tape and yanked it upward. She no longer cared about being careful.

"You shouldn't be there!" a shrill voice

shouted from up near the motel. Suzie froze. Mary spun around looking for the source of the voice. "Yes, you two! You shouldn't be there!" the voice said again.

"Who is that?" Suzie questioned as she turned around to scrutinize the motel. A small figure stepped out from the shadows.

"I know you're not supposed to be there, you're no kind of police," the person accused.

Suzie narrowed her eyes. She could barely see the person beneath a heavy coat and low, floppy hat. What she could see made it clear that the person might not want to be seen. The coat was stained and threadbare. The person's shoes were barely held together with what looked like some duct tape.

"We're just looking," Suzie said in a clear, calm voice. "We're not causing any trouble."

"Trouble, nothing but trouble," the person muttered. As the figure took a few steps closer,

Suzie could tell that it was a woman.

"I'm looking for the missing boat," Suzie explained.

"Suzie, don't tell her what we're doing," Mary warned. "She looks unstable."

"Maybe she saw something," Suzie hissed back. In her time as an investigative reporter she had learned that the invisible people, such as the homeless, children, or those working behind the scenes, usually knew a lot more than expected.

"The boat?" the woman repeated. "That poor fellow," she sighed.

Suzie's heart jumped up into her throat. She was certain now that the woman had seen something.

"What fellow?" she asked as she slipped under the yellow tape and moved closer to the woman.

"Well, it was three men," the woman said and smoothed down her coat which was far too heavy to be wearing in the balmy weather. "But only one was sad. The others were angry."

"There were two men with him?" Suzie pressed. "Do you know why they were angry?"

"There's no drugs here," she barked so loudly that Mary jumped back.

"See," Mary said under her breath. "She doesn't know what she's talking about."

"You hush," the woman glared at Mary before looking back at Suzie. "The poor fellow was so sad. He tried to get away. But they wouldn't let him. They made him get back on the boat."

"You saw all of this?" Suzie asked. "Did you tell the police?"

"Trouble, nothing but trouble," the woman shook her head. "They would make me move. You're not going to tell, are you?" she asked with wide, tired eyes.

"No," Suzie said softly. "I won't tell."

She knew that the woman wouldn't be taken

very seriously as a witness, but she also didn't want the woman to lose the only home she had.

"Good, good," the woman nodded. "Poor fellow," she cleared her throat.

"Did the men hurt him?" Suzie asked breathlessly.

"Sure," the woman nodded. "Pow, pow!" she swung her hands wildly through the air, causing both Mary and Suzie to duck. "But no bangs," the woman sighed with relief. "Guns, but no bangs."

"What about names?" Mary asked. "Did anyone say anyone's name?"

"Just angry words," the woman shook her head and lowered her voice. "Foul words."

Suzie was still recovering from the revelation that there were guns involved. She took comfort in the woman saying that they hadn't been fired, but she also knew that if at any time there was a gun involved in an assault there was a high chance of it being used.

"Did they say where they were going?" Suzie asked hopefully. "The poor fellow, he's my friend, I need to find him."

"Oh, so sorry," the woman said sadly, and seemed to have genuine sympathy in her eyes. "He was so sad."

"But did they say anything about a place they might be headed?" Mary asked quickly. Suzie was still staring warmly into the woman's eyes. She had provided Suzie the one thing she needed the most, the certainty that at one point recently Paul was still alive.

"Out to sea," the woman shrugged and pointed to the wide expanse of the ocean. "Could be anywhere, hmm?" she shook her head. "Poor fellow."

Suzie reached into her purse. She pulled out some cash from her wallet. She didn't have much but what the woman had provided was priceless.

"Are you safe?" she asked as she handed the

woman the money. "Do you need a place to stay?"

"My palace," the woman pointed at the motel. "Don't need nothing really," she eyed the money hesitantly. "It's okay, I don't need that."

"Take it," Suzie encouraged her. "Maybe you could get some shoes?"

"Sure," the woman nodded and took the money. "Thanks," she glanced between Suzie and Mary. "Don't worry I won't tell. Just don't tell on me."

"We won't," Mary promised her.

"I hope you find that sad fellow," the woman muttered as she walked back up towards the motel. She disappeared in the shadows surrounding the old building. Suzie wondered for a moment how long she might have lived there, uninterrupted until Paul's boat showed up. Then her mind returned to Paul.

"I knew it, he was abducted," Suzie said quickly as she walked back towards the police tape. "That means he might still be alive."

"Suzie, I believe Paul is still alive, but you know this woman might not be very trustworthy. She knew the police were here looking for a boat. She might have just made up a story about seeing three men," she paused a moment, knowing that Suzie might not want to hear that.

"I thought of that," Suzie admitted. "But it's the best lead we have right now. The only one really. So, we need to use it. If Paul was here, on the sand, he might have left something behind," she said softly and began looking down at the sand. "To think that he was here, not long ago, probably hoping for help," she whispered, her heart breaking. She pulled her fingers through the sand and felt something hard beneath it. She pulled it up out of the sand and stared at it strangely.

"This doesn't belong here," Suzie murmured.

Mary looked at what she was holding up. It

was a seashell with rose stripes and a scalloped edge.

"It's a seashell, of course it belongs here," Mary said with confusion. "There are probably thousands of shells along this beach."

"But not this one," Suzie argued. "This one I found on a secluded beach that Paul and I visited together. I gave him this shell to remember our time there. He must have dropped it, to let me know that he was here."

"Oh, that's a good sign," Mary said with excitement.

"I bet Paul left this here for me, as a clue to where he was going next," Suzie said, her excitement growing. "He might be at this very beach! I need to go out there," she added with certainty. "Paul left this here for me, I just know it."

"Suzie, I think you're onto something, but how are we going to get there?" Mary pointed out.

"It's not accessible by anything but a boat, right?"

"That's what Paul said when he took me out there," Suzie sighed and shook her head. "I don't know any of his friends well enough to ask them. Besides, it's already getting around town that Paul is a suspect, so I'm sure not many will want to be involved."

"There has to be a way," Mary frowned. "Maybe we could charter one?"

Suzie looked out over the water. She remembered seeing the police boat zip across the waves. "That's it!" she suddenly said. She whipped out her cell phone and dialed Jason's number. He answered on the first ring.

"Jason, I need you to do something for me," she said before he could even speak.

"What?" Jason asked warily.

"I need you to take me out to a certain patch of beach. It's not accessible by land. I'm pretty sure that Paul left me a clue, and I want to follow it," Suzie explained practically all in one breath.

"Suzie, slow down," he said quickly. "What do you mean you found a clue?"

"It was a seashell in the sand," Suzie began to explain.

"There are plenty of seashells in the sand," Jason interrupted her.

"I know that, Jason," Suzie said with exasperation. "But this is a special shell. We found them on this particular strip of beach. Paul said they were only found on that beach."

"It might be a special shell, Suzie, but it's still just a shell," Jason pointed out grimly.

"Jason, are you going to help me or not?" Suzie demanded with frustration. "There is a witness that saw Paul being forced onto the boat by two men."

"What witness?" he asked quickly. "Have you reported it to Parish PD?" he asked.

"No, and I'm not going to," Suzie said sternly. "It doesn't matter who the witness is. They'll just twist it into Paul being a criminal. What if they catch up with him? Do you think they're going to ask questions or shoot first?"

"Suzie," Jason sighed. "I think we need to talk about this in person. I'll meet you at Dune House in an hour. Okay?"

"Yes," Suzie said with a frown. She was hoping it would be sooner, but she wasn't going to get anywhere without a boat.

"And Suzie, don't do anything until we talk," Jason warned her. "You're dealing with Parish PD, if they get wind that you are withholding evidence of some kind they could lock you up for obstruction of justice. Just go back to Dune House and stay there until I get there, understand?"

Suzie raised an eyebrow. She wasn't used to Jason being so forceful. But that only made it clear to her that he was worried about what might happen.

"I understand," she agreed and hung up the phone. She pressed the shell between her fingers and closed her eyes. "What I wouldn't give to be psychic," she sighed as she opened her eyes again. "Jason wants us to meet him at Dune House."

"Remember there was a police officer there?" Mary said as they walked back towards the car. "Do you think he will still be there?"

"I don't know," Suzie frowned. "I hope not."

Chapter Seven

When Suzie and Mary pulled into the long, open driveway that led up the hill to Dune House, the Parish PD cruiser was still sitting in front of the porch. Suzie cringed as she knew that this might not end well.

"Remember, Mary, no mention of the woman we talked to on the beach, okay?" she asked with a frown.

"I remember," Mary nodded nervously. "I just hope it isn't that..."

"Hello ladies," Officer Brown said as he walked up to the car. They hadn't even climbed out yet. "You two are hard to pin down," he said as he opened Mary's door for her. Suzie jerked her door open and glared over the top of the car at the police officer.

"I didn't think I needed to be easy to find," she said.

"Well, I thought you might be a little concerned about your boyfriend," Officer Brown pointed out, his voice growing colder with every word he spoke. "Unless of course, you already know that he is safe."

"How would I know that?" Suzie asked as she walked around the front of the car to stand beside Mary.

"Maybe you're hiding him," Officer Brown suggested as he studied her. "Maybe you think love is more important than a man's life."

"Paul didn't kill anyone," Suzie said gruffly. "He is a good man. I am not hiding him."

"But you wouldn't tell me if you were, would you?" he asked as he held Suzie's bright blue gaze with his own penetrating glare. "So, how do I know you're not lying to me?"

"I guess you don't," Suzie replied coolly.

"Suzie," Mary grabbed her hand and gave it a light squeeze. "Officer Brown we have no idea where Paul is. We've been looking for him, that's why we were not here."

"But that's our job," Officer Brown growled. "Your job is to be in contact with me, so that if something comes up we can discuss it."

"Did something come up?" Suzie asked as she pulled her hand from Mary's and folded her arms across her stomach. She was not going to be intimidated by a man who she believed did not care either way if Paul was alive.

"Paul's boat was spotted by the coast guard this morning down near Sunray Point," Officer Brown explained. "By the time we arrived however, his boat was gone. That should be impossible, considering the coast guard knows every inch of the coast."

Suzie had to press her lips together to keep from laughing. She knew that Paul was familiar with plenty of places that the coast guard would be hard pressed to find.

"What a mystery," she managed to say. "Now, you can see that he is obviously not trying to run away like a guilty person would. He is in danger, and needs help."

"I don't see that at all," Officer Brown argued. "What I see is a desperate man, who came back to the town he was familiar with, not far from your fine establishment here. Maybe he was expecting you to hide him away inside the bed and breakfast?" he suggested.

"Paul would never do anything to put Suzie in danger," Mary snapped. It was clear that she was getting frustrated with the police officer's attitude as well.

"Then you shouldn't mind if I take a look around inside?" the officer inquired.

"Do you have a warrant?" Suzie asked and raised an eyebrow.

Officer Brown's expression grew even angrier. "I didn't expect I would need one," he shot back.

"Well, I'm sorry, Sir, but the privacy of our guests is very important to us," Suzie said, ignoring the fact that they didn't actually have any guests at the B&B at the moment. "Unless you have a warrant that says you have the right to conduct a search then I'm afraid I am going to have to refuse you."

"I can't say that reassures me of your innocence, Ms. Allen," he said and shook his head. "I hope you two haven't gotten yourself into something that you can't handle."

Suzie stared hard at him and did not say another word.

"Is there anything else, officer?" Mary asked as she looped her arm through Suzie's.

"Not just yet," he replied. "But I'm sure we'll be speaking again."

"I'm sure," Suzie replied. "When Paul is home safe and sound and you look like a fool for hunting him like a criminal!"

"Suzie," Mary groaned.

"I hope for your sake, that's the case," Officer Brown said in a sharp tone. Then he stalked off to his car.

"Suzie, you shouldn't have talked to him like that," Mary shook her head as the cruiser took off down the driveway.

"Oh, I know," she said with a huff. "But I have to stand up for Paul, don't I?"

"I suppose so," Mary said with a worried frown. "I just hope we find Paul soon, before we all end up behind bars."

"Don't worry, Mary," Suzie said as she looked at her friend with a warm smile. "I've been there before, we can handle it."

"Nope, not me," Mary said firmly as they walked up the steps to the porch. "I'll make us some lunch, and something for Jason," she said as she disappeared into the house. Suzie rested her hands on the railing and looked out over the water. She couldn't imagine eating anything without knowing if Paul was having a chance to eat. She was still staring out over the water when Jason pulled up. He parked his cruiser and stepped out of the car. Suzie was relieved to see that he didn't have his new partner with him.

"All right, Suzie, maybe you can tell me what is going on now?" he asked. He seemed a little ruffled.

"Is something wrong, Jason?" Suzie asked as he joined her on the porch.

"I just had to lie to my boss to persuade him to let me use the boat," he said grimly. "It's not something I like to do."

"You got the boat?" Suzie asked happily.

"You said you needed it, didn't you?" he asked as he met her eyes. "But we can't use it until later this afternoon."

"What?" Suzie asked. She was getting more frustrated by the moment. "But Paul could be anywhere by then!"

"Suzie, what did you expect me to do, steal it?" Jason frowned. "It's in use for marine patrol until this afternoon."

Suzie sighed and nodded. "I know, I'm sorry, Jason. I just can't believe that someone took him. What could they want from him?"

"I don't know," Jason shook his head. "But I can tell you this," he paused a moment and lowered his voice. "I couldn't leave it alone, so I ran Trent's name through the system. Turns out it is a false identity. I also had a friend of mine in another department run Trent's driver's license photograph through a facial recognition program and we got no matches."

Suzie's eyes widened at his words. She hadn't expected him to do so much, especially after the spat Jason and Paul had over breakfast. "Did he find anything?" she asked.

"Not much," Jason replied. "Not even a name.

96

But there is absolutely no record of him ever working as a deckhand before. I have a feeling he didn't get on the boat to earn some money from Paul. He must have had other intentions."

"Other intentions," Suzie repeated softly. Her mind was spinning as she processed the new information.

"Jason, good to see you," Mary said as she stepped out onto the porch. "Are you hungry?"

"Starving," Jason replied with a sigh of relief.

"Come inside and eat something," she suggested. "You look like you've lost even more weight," she chastised. Jason was slender to begin with.

"I've been running," he admitted.

"Must be that new girlfriend," Mary said with a slight smile.

"Ah well," Jason blushed almost as red as his hair.

"How is Dr. Rose?" Mary asked.

"Dr. Rose," Suzie repeated interrupting their conversation. "Is she working the case?"

"Most likely," Jason replied, relieved to have the topic changed. "Parish uses her on most criminal cases because she has the most experience in forensics."

"I want to go see Trent's body," Suzie said sternly.

"Do you really think that's a good idea?" Mary asked hesitantly.

"If Paul left the shell for me to find, then maybe there is another clue on Trent's body," Suzie pointed out. "We already know that Trent isn't who he claimed to be. We know he wasn't on that boat to work for Paul. So, we need to figure out what he was doing there, and who he was. If we find that out, we might be able to predict where Paul has been taken."

"I don't know," Jason frowned.

"If we can't get out on the water until this afternoon, I have to do something." Suzie said as she locked eyes with him.

"Suzie, I can't really get involved," Jason began to say.

"No, you can't get involved," Suzie agreed. "But I can, and I'm going to, with or without your help, Jason."

"All right," he nodded and pulled out his cell phone. "I'll give her a call and find out. But I can't promise you that she'll let you in."

"I'm sure you can work something out," Mary said with a slightly hidden smile. Jason flicked his eyes in her direction as if he'd been caught in some kind of criminal act. Before he could question what she meant, he turned away.

"Hey it's Jason. I know you're busy. Are you working the Trent Baker case?" he asked. He nodded a little as she replied. "Right well, I'm not working the case, it's not in our jurisdiction, but it involves Paul. Suzie wanted to know if she could come take a look at the remains."

He paused and reached up to scratch at the back of his neck. "I know it's against procedure," he agreed and glanced over at Suzie. "Great, okay I'll tell her," he continued, his tone of voice giving no hint of her response. He cleared his throat and turned away from the two women again.

"Love you, too," he murmured before hanging up the phone.

"What did she say?" Suzie asked. Mary's eyes were wide as she had overheard what Jason said.

"She said you can come take a look, but you have to be in and out, and you can't touch the body," Jason said sternly.

"And that she loves you," Mary added with a sweet smile.

"None of that," Jason warned as he wagged a finger at Mary.

"How long have you been dating?" Suzie

asked with surprise. "Isn't it a little soon to be saying things like that?"

Jason blushed again. "I guess not, if it's what you feel," he mumbled. "I'll be back later to take you out on the boat," he added and hurried down the steps.

"But Jason, your lunch!" Mary called out.

"I have to go," Jason hollered back before taking off in his cruiser.

"He just didn't want us to grill him," Mary huffed.

"Don't you find it a little bit odd that they are already saying those things?" Suzie asked.

"Not really," Mary shrugged. "Kent told me on our second date," she rolled her eyes. "Not that he meant it."

Suzie frowned. She had no question in her mind that she loved Paul, but she had never dared to say it. Now, she might never have the chance.

"I'm going to see Trent's body," Suzie said and started down the steps.

"But lunch?" Mary called out. Suzie was already at the car.

"Save me something?" Suzie asked with an apologetic frown.

"Sure," Mary nodded and sighed as she stepped back into Dune House.

Chapter Eight

Suzie had visited a Medical Examiner's Office a few times before but it wasn't a place that she preferred to frequent. She was always surprised by how stark it was. Everything was very clean. Everything smelled like chemicals and disinfectant. Even the receptionist who greeted Suzie with a scowl.

"Can I help you?" she asked.

"I'm here to see Dr. Rose," Suzie replied.

"Sorry, you can't see her like that," the woman said with a sneer.

Suzie looked down at her jeans and button up shirt. She didn't see anything wrong with it.

"Excuse me?" she asked. "Why not?"

"You're breathing," the receptionist replied. She stared sternly at Suzie. Suzie was confused until the woman erupted into loud laughter that echoed through the otherwise quiet room.

"It's a joke, you know," she laughed louder. "Only the dead get in," she continued to giggle.

Suzie could only stare at her, her mouth half-open. Had she been in a better mood she might have laughed. As it was she had no idea how to respond.

The door beside the desk opened and Dr. Rose stepped out.

"Are you telling jokes again, Sharon?" she asked as the receptionist finally muffled her laughter.

"I don't think she got it," Sharon said glumly.

"I'm sorry, Suzie, things get a little tense around here, so Sharon likes to lighten them up," Dr. Rose offered a small smile.

"It was a good joke," Suzie said and offered a quiet laugh to appease Sharon who had returned to her sullen expression. She wasn't someone that Suzie would expect to try and brighten things up, but obviously there was more to Sharon than she realized.

"I'll take you back," Dr. Rose said and held the door open for Suzie. As Suzie walked through it she felt the temperature drop considerably. It was a little unsettling to walk into a place where she knew dead bodies were waiting to be examined.

"Trent's over here," Dr. Rose said. "Are you sure that you're up for this?" she asked.

"I'm sure," Suzie replied, though she wasn't sure at all. Nervously she followed after Dr. Rose.

The body was sprawled out across a gurney with a sheet covering everything but his head and neck. Suzie shivered a little as she looked at it. It was never easy to face mortality. She hadn't liked Trent but that didn't mean she wished him dead. But Paul was in trouble. She had to figure out where he was, and if it meant facing Trent's remains, then she would have to be brave enough to do so.

"Suzie, I'm not sure what you're hoping to find," Dr. Rose said as she brushed her dark blond hair back over her shoulders. "I've already done the initial exam."

"Is there anything you can tell me?" Suzie asked. "Is there any sign that can clear Paul?"

"Actually," Dr. Rose frowned. "I'm sorry, Suzie, but the killer was right handed, as is Paul. From the evidence left on the body it's clear that Paul had close contact with Trent. I even found a few hairs that match Paul's color and texture on Trent's shoulder."

"You know he didn't do this, don't you?" Suzie asked incredulously.

"It isn't my job to know who did what," Dr. Rose said firmly. "It's my job to report my findings. Based on the angle of the blows it is possible that the murderer was a similar height to Paul as well. Trust me, I'm not pinpointing Paul, but I am reporting my findings."

"If it was Paul, then it must have been in self-defense," Suzie said anxiously. "He must have been under attack."

"There isn't any evidence to indicate that Trent was the attacker, but there isn't any evidence to dispute it either," Dr. Rose frowned. "I will know more once the tox screens come back, and I'm able to process some DNA I found underneath Trent's fingernails."

Suzie's stomach flipped. She wondered what would happen if that DNA came back to match Paul's. Trent had clawed at Paul's hand when he was holding him up against the wall. There was little doubt in her mind that Paul's DNA would be there. But she also knew that Paul hadn't done this. She didn't think he could, even if he was threatened.

"What about his clothes?" Suzie asked quickly. "Did you find anything in his pockets, or anything like that?"

"There was something," Dr. Rose said with a slight frown. She picked up one of the evidence bags on the metal table next to her. "It wasn't in his pocket, but it was around his neck. Are you familiar with this symbol?" she asked as she met Suzie's eyes.

Suzie studied the gold necklace inside the plastic bag. The pendant that hung from it looked similar to a medal that would represent a saint. However, instead of there being any kind of religious symbol there was a swirl in the shape of an uppercase A.

"No," Suzie said as she narrowed her eyes. "Should I be?"

"Not necessarily," Dr. Rose said as she set the bag down. "The A represents a gang in Los Angeles. It's not a very well-known one, but I have heard of some very ruthless murders that these gang members are involved in. I'm only telling you this, because I want you to understand that Paul likely had no idea who he was getting onto that boat with. Like I said, I have to report the evidence, but if Trent was involved with this gang, then he was likely a very dangerous man."

Suzie felt sick to her stomach, not just because of the chemical smell. If Trent was such a dangerous man, what did that say about the men who had killed him and were now holding Paul hostage?

"Thank you, Dr. Rose," Suzie said with a frown. She left the medical examiner's office without much more certainty than she had entered with. But at least she had a lead on who Trent might actually be.

Chapter Nine

When Suzie returned to Dune House she noticed the door to Mary's room was closed, which meant she was likely taking a nap. Mary hadn't slept much the night before either. As tired as Suzie was she couldn't wait to get in front of her computer. She wanted to find out about the gang that Trent was associated with. After a little bit of searching she came across some information about them. Dr. Rose had been correct, they had a reputation for being especially violent and ruthless. But that wasn't the only information Suzie found. She also discovered that their main criminal activity was dealing in drugs.

Suzie suddenly recalled what the woman on the beach had said. She had dismissed it as just a little ranting and raving from an unclear mind, but now she realized that the woman had been trying to answer her question. The men who had

Paul must have been looking for drugs. It all began to snap together and make sense to Suzie.

"Suzie?" a voice called out from the hallway. "Jason's here," Mary said.

Suzie closed her computer and nearly ran out into the hall. Mary still looked a little sleepy as she followed after Suzie. They met Jason in the front hall.

"Jason, I think I've figured out just what Trent was doing on that boat, and why those men are holding Paul hostage," she said breathlessly before Jason could even greet her.

"Wow, that's a lot of police work," Jason said and blinked. "Could you start from the beginning for me?"

"Trent is associated with a gang that's known for dealing drugs. He didn't have any history of being a deckhand, but he wanted to get on Paul's boat badly. Why would he want to get on the boat? To transport drugs of course!" Suzie said with a snap of her fingers. "So, he gets on the boat with Paul, who has no idea what he's in for. But then something goes wrong. The deal goes bad, or Paul finds out what Trent is up to, who knows. But something happened that caused those men to kill Trent."

"Okay," Jason said slowly as he followed her thought process. "So, if Trent hid the drugs, then they are likely looking for the drugs. With Trent dead their only hope is if Paul can lead them to the drugs."

"Yes," Suzie said quickly. "Does it make sense now?" she asked with wide eyes.

"It does," Jason admitted.

"But there's one problem," Mary said in a whisper.

"What?" Jason asked.

"Paul wouldn't know where the drugs are, because he would never be involved in such a thing," she frowned.

"You're right," Suzie said, her spirits falling. "Paul's clever enough to lead those men on for a while, but eventually they're going to figure out that he doesn't know where the drugs are."

"Then we need to find him before they do," Mary said with determination. "Is the boat ready?"

Jason nodded. "We only have it for a short time though."

"That's fine, I know exactly where we are going," Suzie said.

The three piled into Jason's police cruiser. He drove them to the marina where the boat was prepped and ready to launch. Jason helped Suzie and Mary onto the boat and then took the helm.

"Are you sure you know how to do this, Jason?" Mary asked nervously.

"Don't worry, Mary, I've taken it out several times," Jason assured her. "It's part of our training."

"Okay," Mary replied and tried to make her smile look a little more confident.

Suzie was staring out across the water. She was willing herself to see Paul, despite the distance separating them. The boat rocked as Jason headed out to sea.

"Can you go faster?" she asked him.

Jason shook his head. "I'm going as fast as I can," he replied. Suzie instructed him where to maneuver the boat.

"I didn't even know this inlet existed," Jason said with amazement as he followed her directions.

"And we need to keep it that way," Suzie said firmly. "It's one of Paul's sacred places."

"My lips are sealed," Jason said.

"Here," Suzie said and pointed to the shore. "I'll have to wade in."

"No need," Jason said as he pulled the boat

right up to shore. "It's equipped to dry dock," he explained.

Jason, Suzie, and Mary made their way off the boat. The beach was as barren as Suzie recalled it being. In the distance she heard Bonnie Blue's mournful cry. Her heart ached as she wondered if Paul would have the chance to hear it again.

"I'll stay with the boat," Jason said. "If you find anything call me," he paused a moment. "If you see anyone, I mean anyone, Suzie, call me right away. Don't approach anyone. If Paul is really being held by these criminals then they are ruthless enough to hurt anyone they see."

"I'll be careful," Suzie assured him.

"We'll be careful," Mary corrected gently and fell into step beside Suzie. Suzie made her way along the sand. She was getting more disappointed by the moment. There was no evidence of any struggle on the beach. There was no sign that anyone had even been there since the last time they had visited. She took a deep breath and traced her fingertips along her forehead.

"Think, Suzie," she said to herself. "Why would Paul lead you here?"

Suzie presumed that the only reason Paul would have left her the clue of the seashell was to guide her to his next destination. But the question remained, had he made it? Was the seashell even a clue in the first place?

"This way," she said softly to Mary as they made their way out to the private patch of beach that Paul had shared with her.

"It's so beautiful," Mary said as she drank in the tiny paradise. Bonnie Blue was perched in her usual spot. She turned her head towards Suzie as Suzie approached. Then she wailed and took flight.

"I know, Bonnie," Suzie said softly to herself. "I miss him, too."

Suzie began searching the site for anything

that Paul might have left as a clue. Or even just proof that he had been there at all. Mary searched right along with her but as the afternoon sun beat down on them, she shook her head.

"Suzie, I don't think there's anything here," she said softly.

"There has to be," Suzie said firmly. Her phone began to ring. She knew it was Jason calling them back to the boat. She ignored it. "I can't leave here without something," she gasped out.

"Even if he was here, Suzie, there's no guarantee that he left something," Mary explained in a rational tone. "I think it's time we told Officer Brown what we think. Let the police search this area..."

"No," Suzie said firmly. "They won't look for Paul to help him, they just want to arrest him. I can't let that happen. I have to catch those criminals that took him."

"Suzie," Mary said in a softer voice. "There's nothing here but sand. Besides we have guests coming in tonight and..." she gasped as she nearly lost her balance. Her foot had caught on the edge of something sticking up out of the sand. Suzie lunged forward to grab Mary by the arm before she could fall forward into the sand.

"Mary, are you okay?" she asked urgently.

"I think so," Mary muttered as she straightened herself up. "I wasn't expecting to fall, that's for sure."

"Did you trip on something?" Suzie asked with a frown.

"Yes, must have been a big shell or something," she looked down around her feet.

"That's no shell," Suzie said as she spotted what was sticking up out of the sand. It was a pocket-sized leather book. She plucked the book out of the sand. "I know this book," she said in a whisper. "This is Paul's log book. He keeps track of his every movement in here when he's out to sea."

"How do you think it got here?" Mary asked with fascination.

"He had to have left it," Suzie said quickly. "Look, it's not wet or anything. It couldn't have washed ashore. The way it was buried in the sand means that he was trying to hide it."

"How would he be able to hide it?" Mary asked with confusion.

"Paul is a brave and brilliant man," Suzie said with determination. "He is trying his hardest to make sure that someone finds him. I am willing to bet that his last entry in this log book is where he and his captors went next. We have to go there, now," she said sternly.

"But Jason said we have to go back with the boat," Mary began to say.

"Paul is very clever, he's a survivor, he would do whatever he had to do to leave a trail so that someone could find him," she held the log book tightly in her hand. "I am going to find him."

Mary was staring up and down the long beach. "But where did he go?" she asked softly.

"I can find it," Suzie said with confidence. "Paul had me download an application for my phone that will accept coordinates and give directions."

Her phone began to ring again. Suzie finally answered it.

"Suzie, we're already late, you're going to get me fired," Jason said with frustration when she answered.

"Jason, Mary's on her way. I'm going to stay out here for a while," she locked eyes with Mary. "I just need some time to calm down and relax."

"I think that's a good idea, Suzie," Jason said. "I'm sorry that you didn't find what you were looking for."

"I'm sorry, too," Suzie replied. "Can I call you

to get a ride back when I'm ready?"

"I can take the boat back out around sunset," he replied. "That's the next patrol. Make sure you're ready then, okay?"

"I will," Suzie agreed.

"I'm sorry, Suzie," Jason said with a sigh. "I'm sure Paul will turn up soon."

Suzie couldn't answer. Her throat had gone dry with worry. Was she going to be too late to save Paul?

"Suzie, I don't want to leave without you," Mary said. She was looking nervously out at the water. "You aren't going after those terrible men are you?"

"I'm just going to see if I can find the location. If I check it out and there's reason to believe that Paul left it as a clue I'll call Jason and let him know," she promised. "I don't want to waste police time on what could be a wild goose chase."

"Still, I'd feel better if I stayed," Mary argued.

"Remember the guests?" Suzie said. "It's their first time away from the baby. They need this to be perfect. Only you can make it perfect."

Mary sighed. "Fine but don't stay out here long. If anything even feels funny, call Jason. Promise me?"

"I promise," Suzie said firmly. Mary reached out and hugged her. Then she reluctantly walked back towards Jason and the boat. Suzie tapped the coordinates into her phone. She waited for the program to generate the location. As she had hoped it was along the same inlet. She would be able to walk to it. She began walking in the right direction. With every step she felt her excitement growing. She was sure that she was going to find Paul at any second. Her heart was racing.

The directions led her through a wooded area. As she emerged on the other side, she caught sight of something glimmering in the water. As she crept out a little farther she could see that it was Paul's boat. Her heart soared as she stared at the boat. Paul was there. He had to be. A little further down the beach she spotted a small shack. It was completely exposed. Suzie guessed that Paul was either on the boat or in that shack. But she also had to anticipate that he wasn't alone. If he was, he would have called for help already. She had to fight the urge to go running towards the boat. She knew it wouldn't help Paul if she were to be captured as well.

Suzie took a breath and formed a plan. She would try to get to the boat first. With any luck Paul would be on it, and the criminals that had held him hostage would be long gone. Maybe he was tied up and not able to use his radio. Maybe, though she hoped it wasn't the case, he was injured and unable to move. She didn't allow herself to think of any other possibility.

"I'm here, Paul," she whispered, though she knew that he couldn't hear her. To get to the boat she would be slightly exposed. Suzie guessed it would be her best bet to get to the water and then wade towards the boat. If the criminals spotted her she could at least dive under the water. As she walked down towards the edge of the water, her body was tense with fear. She recalled the information she had read about the gang that Trent was affiliated with. If they spotted her they wouldn't hesitate to shoot.

"No bangs," she remembered the woman saying when she had described what she had seen during Paul's struggle with his captors. But that was only because they wanted Paul alive. They wouldn't care about having another body to add to their tally. In the distance she thought she heard Bonnie Blue's call.

"He'll be back soon," she whispered more to encourage herself than to appease the bird. Suzie took off her shoes and held them in her hand as she walked into the water. She walked far enough in that she could walk directly to the boat. The water almost came up to her knees but she was too scared to feel the cold of it. Her pants were soaked through as she waded through the water as quickly as possible while keeping an eager eye out for any sign of Paul or the criminals.

When she finally reached the boat, she could hear the slosh of the waves against the side of the boat. She listened closely, but she didn't hear any sounds coming from inside the boat. In her mind she willed Paul to be okay, and to know that he was going to be rescued. Cautiously she crept closer to the boat. She held her breath as the water sloshed and swirled around her feet. At least the sound of the waves served to drown out what she thought had to be the loudest her heart had ever pounded.

A few more steps took her to the side of the boat. The sun was low in the sky, so the boat cast a shadow that hid her slightly from view. She crouched down beside the boat. When she did, the boat rocked, and made a long, low creaking sound. She tensed as she wondered if it would alert the criminals. She still wasn't sure where they were. She still didn't hear any sounds coming from the boat. As she tried to work up the courage to look inside the boat, she was startled by a voice.

"Be on the look out, it has to be out there somewhere," the distorted voice said.

After a terrifying moment Suzie realized that the voice was carrying over the radio in Paul's boat. It was likely chatter from the coast guard or other boaters that were looking for Paul's boat. She took a deep breath to steady her nerves and waited to see if anyone would speak on the boat. When no one did she relaxed slightly. Suzie could see the dilapidated shack from where she was crouched down beside Paul's boat. She thought about climbing on to it, to use his radio to call for the coast guard. But she was afraid that there might still be someone hiding inside it.

Suzie also knew that the police would not be looking out for Paul's best interest as he was still considered the prime suspect in Trent's murder. If she was spotted climbing onto the boat by Paul's captors it would mean she wouldn't survive, and more than likely neither would Paul. At the moment she had the element of surprise on her side. She pulled out her cell phone and attempted to send Jason a text. She told him that she had found Paul's boat and that she thought he was being held hostage. She included the coordinates and the best description of her location that she could muster. But when she hit send, the text was delayed because of lack of service.

"Shoot," she muttered to herself as she tucked her phone back into her pocket. She was shocked into silence when she heard some shouting from inside the shack. She was too far away to understand what was being said, but the tone of voice was threatening. Between herself and the shack was a long open strip of sand. The moment she stepped out onto it she would be fully exposed.

Suzie drew a deep breath in and looked at her surroundings. The tree line was not far off, but she would have to pass the shack to get to it. Her only chance was to run as fast as she could. Beside the boat she was a sitting duck. If the criminals decided to walk out to the boat, she would be seen right away. After some careful thought the best choice seemed to be to run. She waited until she heard the shouting again. Whoever was holding Paul captive would be less likely to see her coming if they were busy screaming. Once the shouting started, Suzie bolted as fast as she could across the sand. Her heart pounded as she wondered if she would make it.

Suddenly, she heard a loud, sharp noise, the sound of a bullet being fired. She braced herself, thinking that she was about to experience being shot.

Chapter Ten

After a few seconds of no pain, Suzie realized the bullet had not been fired at her. She was at the edge of the shack. Now that she was close enough, she could hear what was happening inside. Paul's captor was shouting again.

"That was a warning," a disgruntled voice said. "The next one will be aimed at you if you don't tell me where the drugs are."

"I thought they were here," Paul insisted. "Maybe Trent moved them. This is where they were supposed to be."

Suzie was a little shocked by his words, but overjoyed to hear his voice. After a moment of elation, she had a terrible thought. What if Paul really had known about the drugs? What if he was trying to make some extra money and didn't think it would be too much of a risk? It was a terrible thing to think. She pushed the thought from her mind.

"You've fooled us one too many times," the man shouted. "First you said the drugs were by the motel, then you told us that they were somewhere else, and now finally we're here where you swore the drugs were hidden, and you're lying to us again."

"I'm not lying," Paul said mournfully. "They should have been here. Maybe they are hidden in those woods."

"No more maybes! I told you that we shouldn't have killed Trent until we had the drugs," another voice said with irritation.

"This guy is supposed to be his partner, he must know where the drugs are," the first voice growled.

"Obviously he doesn't," the second voice snapped back. "Trent was playing all of us, what makes you think he wasn't playing this guy, too?"

"Well, if he was, he's of no use to us, now," the

first voice said with a grunt. "He's nothing but a liability. He doesn't know where the drugs are. If we don't find them, it's our lives on the line."

Suzie tensed when she heard those words. She knew that if Paul wasn't worth anything to them, he would never get out of there alive. There were only moments to intervene.

"All right," she heard Paul finally say. "I give in, I know where the drugs are," he admitted.

"See," the first voice said. "All it takes is a little persuasion. So, where are they?" he demanded.

"I can't tell you, I have to show you," Paul explained.

"Another story that he's making up to save his skin?" the second voice said. "I don't trust it, he could be setting us up."

"For what? A swim with the sharks?" the first voice asked. "This place is isolated, no one else is on this beach. He's got nowhere to run, nowhere to hide. If he lies to us, he dies. Do you hear that?"

he shouted. "If you play a game with me you will regret it!"

Suzie crept closer to the window of the shack. She was so close that it seemed as if the men were shouting right beside her ear. She peered inside to see Paul tied to an old wooden chair. His hands were bound behind his back, and his feet were duct taped to the legs of the chair. There was no way that he could escape.

"I think he's lying right now," the second voice growled. "If he knew where the drugs were he would have told us already."

"I don't care what you think, I'm not going back to the boss with nothing to show," the first voice snapped. Both of the men were burly, and they wore torn t-shirts paired with ratty shorts. It seemed that they were familiar with the criminal life as they commanded Paul with ease and authority. Suzie ducked back down as the taller man turned towards the window. Her heart raced as she wondered if he had spotted her.

"Gabriel, we need to get out of here," the second man demanded sharply. "What if the coast guard spots his boat? We could be swarmed with cops any minute and you want to waste time on another one of his lies? We're better off just looking for the drugs ourselves."

"So, what if the cops do come?" Gabriel replied harshly. "Then they'll just find the guy that killed his deckhand. The only question is will he be alive or dead to tell the tale. We're not looking for anything but the drugs, pal. If you give them up, you might get out of this still breathing."

"Like I said, I can't tell you, I have to show you," Paul repeated with determination. "Look I'm doing you both a favor, all of these inlets can be pretty tricky. If you try to find it by yourself you're never going to make it. Let's just get back on the boat and I'll take you where we need to go. You'll see, when we get there, that it was all worth it."

"I don't know," Gabriel said hesitantly.

"You've been jerking us around for quite some time."

"Are you really going to believe this idiot?" his partner asked. "He's going to lead us right into a trap!"

"I just want to live," Paul said calmly. "I'm not ready to call it quits. You just want your drugs, I just want my life. We can do an even exchange, no need for police, or anyone else to get involved," he said firmly. The way he spoke those words made Suzie wonder if he knew she was outside. Had he seen her when she peered in the window? She didn't dare to look again, or she might be spotted by the two men.

"It's risky," Gabriel's partner argued. "If we're on the water the coast guard might see us."

"This whole thing is risky, Joey, that's the point," Gabriel snapped. "If we don't get the drugs, what do you think the boss is going to do to us? A whole lot worse than the cops ever will."

"All right, all right," Joey finally relented. "But I'm staying right next to him the whole time. If he tries anything shady, I'm putting a bullet in his head."

"Fine," Gabriel agreed. "If I don't do it first."

Suzie's stomach twisted with revulsion. They were talking about Paul's life as if it was just another piece of garbage to be tossed aside. There wasn't a trace of remorse in their words.

Suzie heard a blade rip through the duct tape on the legs of the chair. She heard Paul grunt, and wince. Had the blade come too close to his skin?

"Get up," Gabriel barked so loudly that Suzie jumped.

Suzie heard some scuffing of shoes. She knew that Paul was standing up.

"You stay in front of me," Joey demanded. "You feel that?" he asked. "That's a gun in your back. If you try anything funny I will pull the trigger, got it?"

"Got it," Paul's hardened voice replied. Suzie flattened herself against the outside wall of the shack as the three men walked out through the front door.

"You need to tell us where we're going, before we get on the boat," Gabriel said with a growl. "I want to know exactly where or you're not making it off this beach."

"It's about a mile further up the shore," Paul said quickly. "Trent was going to hide the drugs here, but he thought it was too exposed, so we moved them up further where there are a lot of rocks."

"Likely story," Joey growled. "You want to know where I think those drugs are?" he asked with confidence building.

"Fine, genius, where are they?" Gabriel asked impatiently.

"We only know for certain that Trent was in two places. This guy's boat, and that bed and breakfast where he spent the night. My money's on Trent hiding the drugs inside of that old place. It's huge, he'd have plenty of places to hide them. Why would he risk taking them out on the boat when he was already planning on double crossing us?" he demanded.

"No," Paul said quickly. "Not there. They aren't there, I know it. Don't look there," he insisted.

"Actually, he has a good point," Gabriel said. "Maybe Trent just let you think he had the drugs on the boat. It would make sense for him to leave them behind, somewhere he could easily find them when he was ready to take off. He wouldn't be able to drive a boat himself. He wouldn't be able to make it through all the tricky inlets you keep telling us about. I think you're right, Joey, for once. I think those drugs are back at that bed and breakfast."

Suzie's heart stopped beating for a moment. She thought of Mary back at Dune House, all alone with no way to protect herself. If these two men decided to invade it she would be in grave danger. With her cell phone having no service, and no boat to get back to the mainland, Suzie would have no way to warn her. She was certain that if those men got on the boat, it would mean that Mary would be in danger. Not only Mary, but the young couple who were taking their first trip away from their young baby. These men wouldn't care who they killed in order to get their drugs.

"No," Paul said firmly again. "I told you, I know where the drugs are. I can take you to them. It has nothing to do with that place."

"You seem so certain," Joey said slyly. "Almost too certain. Don't you think, Gabriel?" he asked.

"He is acting a little strange," Gabriel said. "Are you still trying to keep those drugs yourself?" he asked Paul sharply.

"No," Paul said again. "Please, I told you. I

just want to live. I don't care about the drugs. I just want to get back home, in one piece, so I can continue with my life. We're on the same side here. I want to take you to those drugs, as much as you want to find them."

"If that was the case you would have told us right away," Joey roared. "Instead you've had us roaming all over this water and this beach looking for something you knew wasn't here. Were you hoping we'd get picked up by the coast guard before you had to part ways with the drugs?" he accused.

"You've got it wrong," Paul insisted. Suzie could hear the panic forming in his voice. He was as worried as she was that the two would end up at Dune House. "If you want your drugs I'll take you to them."

"No," Gabriel said slowly. "I think I'm going to go with Joey on this one. It just makes so much more sense that Trent would hide the drugs there. I think we'll take you along for the ride, and if it turns out the drugs aren't there, then you can bring us back to this other place."

"That's not wise," Paul argued.

"Now, he's advising us," Joey laughed. "This guy's playing us, Gabriel. Let me take him out right here. Then we don't have to worry about getting rid of the body."

With Joey's words, Suzie's panic went into full force. She knew that if she didn't do something, Paul would either end up dead, or they would all end up heading for Dune House and she would be left behind with no way to warn anyone. Without much time to think about what she was doing she stood up and walked around the side of the shack. She walked right through the door, knowing each step might be her last.

Chapter Eleven

"Paul, I've been looking for you everywhere," Suzie said impatiently as she entered the room. Then she fell silent as the two men turned and pointed their guns directly at her. Paul's eyes were wide and filled with horror as he saw Suzie in the line of fire. "Who are they?" she demanded. "Are you trying to cut me out of the deal?"

"Who are you?" Gabriel growled and released the safety on his gun. His finger was pressing lightly on the trigger, just waiting for a reason to push harder.

"I'm his girlfriend," Suzie said breathlessly. "I was supposed to meet him here and..."

"Shut up!" Joey screeched. "This is insane. It's like a circus around here!"

"Who is she?" Gabriel growled sharply at Paul.

"She's uh," Paul hesitated. Suzie knew he was

trying to think of a way to protect her. "She's my partner," he finally said.

"Another partner?" Joey demanded. "I just want the drugs and to get out of this place!"

Gabriel had turned back to glare at Suzie.

"I have the drugs," Suzie said as she stared into Gabriel's eyes.

"What are you talking about?" he demanded. "How could you have the drugs?"

"Trent was staying at my B&B," she explained. "I overheard his plans. I knew that he was going to make a lot of money from double crossing you. I needed some money, so I talked to Paul, and we made a plan together, so that we could sell the drugs ourselves."

"How?" Gabriel asked as he slowly stepped closer to her. As Suzie had hoped he would, Joey turned the gun from Paul, to point it at Suzie.

"Suzie, no," Paul breathed, his eyes wide with fear.

"We waited until Trent put the drugs on the boat, then the plan was that Paul would find out where he was hiding them. Then we were going to get rid of Trent, but you took care of that before we could," she reminded them. "Paul was supposed to move the drugs a few times so Trent would have no idea where they really were. We were going to take a trip," she added wistfully. "Around the world. We were supposed to meet up here, and then go get the drugs from where Paul had hidden them."

Suzie was putting together the ideas so fast that she wasn't sure if they even made sense. She only knew that if she kept talking, then no one was shooting anyone. If she could just buy enough time until Jason came back for her then he might find them and they might have a chance to escape.

Paul's eyes narrowed sharply. Gabriel turned to look at him and waved the gun in front of his face.

"Is this all true?" he demanded. "Is this why

you've been running us all around?"

Paul was silent. Suzie knew that he didn't want her to be involved, but it was too late for that the moment she had stepped inside the shack. He nodded a little and closed his eyes briefly.

"That was a big mistake," Gabriel growled as he turned back and pointed the gun directly in Suzie's face.

"I see that now," she said and swallowed thickly. "I didn't realize what powerful men Trent was working with," she added hoping that a little flattery would ease their anger. "If I had known, I never would have touched the drugs."

Gabriel glared as he took a final step closer to Suzie.

"You should have known better," he growled. "Now, you're both going to pay. You first," he added and his arm tensed.

"No!" Paul shouted. "No, I swear if you shoot her I'll never tell you where your drugs are," he said desperately. "Please, I'll do anything," he added.

Gabriel lowered the gun. "Aw how sweet," he said with annoyance. "A true romantic, willing to give his life for his girlfriend," he turned back and pointed the gun directly in Paul's face. "Let's see if she'll do the same for you, lover boy."

"This is getting out of control," Joey complained. "How are we going to get the drugs if they're dead?"

"We only need one of them alive," Gabriel snapped. "I'm not getting on the boat with both of them. They might try to plan something."

"All right fine," Joey huffed. "Which one do you want me to take out?"

"We need someone to drive the boat," Gabriel reminded Joey as if he was an idiot.

"Oh right," Joey nodded. He grabbed Suzie hard by the arm and started to pull her out of the shack.

"No!" Paul shouted and lunged towards Joey. "No don't!"

Gabriel tackled Paul easily to the ground and placed the gun at his back. "Stay down," he commanded him.

Suzie was in a full panic. She knew the moment Joey got her outside of the shack she would be dead. She realized that no matter how hard she had tried to save Paul, she had failed.

As Joey pulled Suzie out of the shack they nearly collided with Jason who was running up along the beach. He must have heard all of the shouting. Jason drew his gun and aimed it at Joey.

"Drop your gun," he snapped sharply. Suzie could barely take a breath she was so terrified. Jason was now in danger as well. She didn't know if he even knew that Gabriel was inside.

Joey started to raise his gun to point it at Suzie who was struggling hard to escape his grasp. When he did, she was able to lunge a short distance from him. Jason shot him in the shoulder that was holding the gun. Joey cried out in pain and dropped the gun. Suzie quickly picked it up, but her hands were shaking. Jason met her eyes in the same moment that Gabriel emerged from the shack.

"Drop them both or he's dead," Gabriel threatened. Jason had already spun to face Gabriel.

"Lower your weapon," he commanded Gabriel. Gabriel had his arm around Paul's throat and his gun to Paul's head.

"You drop yours," he growled back. "Or this guy's a dead man!"

Suzie was trying desperately to hold onto the gun she was pointing at Joey who was writhing on the ground in pain. Gabriel's threat left her even more terrified. Jason held his gun steadily pointed at Gabriel.

"If you pull that trigger you're going next,"

Jason said sternly. "I don't think you've come this far just to die in the sand."

"You don't know anything about it," Gabriel said in a seething tone. "We're getting on that boat, and if you so much as look in my direction, he goes, and so do you."

"Let him go," Suzie demanded. "Or Joey is going to die."

"You think I care about that?" Gabriel laughed. "We're going to get on the boat," he said again and began pulling Paul towards it.

"There's no way off this beach if you shoot me," Paul struggled to say. "A boat's no good if you don't know how to drive it. Think this through, Gabriel. Handcuffs are a lot better than a watery grave."

"Shut up!" Gabriel insisted. It was clear that he was getting more frustrated and frightened by the moment.

"The coast guard is on its way," Jason warned

him. "The moment you hit the water they will be on top of you. So, how many deaths do you want on your head?" Jason asked. "Because no matter what, you're not getting out of here in anything but handcuffs or a coffin."

"There is no escape," Paul croaked out. "It's over, Gabriel."

"Drop the gun," Jason demanded. "Just drop the gun and put your hands on your head."

The expression on Gabriel's face shifted. It went from anger, to a strange look of serenity. For a moment Suzie was certain that he was going to pull the trigger. He pressed the barrel of the gun hard against the side of Paul's head.

"No," Suzie whispered. "Please don't."

Paul looked into her eyes. He didn't have to speak for her to know what he was saying. Suzie thought that it would be the last moment they would share. Then abruptly Gabriel lowered the gun. He dropped it to the sand beside him.

"Put your hands up," Jason ordered him.

Gabriel reluctantly released Paul and raised his hands into the air. Paul lunged away from him and scooped up the gun that was resting in the sand.

"I'm having a rough day," Gabriel muttered as he placed his hands on the top of his head.

"You aren't the one that got shot!" Joey complained from the ground.

"Get on your knees," Jason commanded him. As he walked around behind Gabriel to handcuff him, Paul rushed over to Suzie. He took the gun from her trembling hands and held it on Joey.

"Are you okay?" he asked her desperately.

"I should be asking you that," she said in a trembling whisper.

"I'm only okay if you are," Paul replied and looked into her eyes intently. "I can't believe you did that."

Jason walked over and cuffed Joey who was still moaning and squirming in the sand. He took the gun from Paul. As Jason spoke into his radio requesting backup, Paul led Suzie further away from the two handcuffed men.

"Suzie, you scared the hell out of me," he said as he grasped her hands tightly. "Why would you ever do something so foolish?"

Suzie frowned as she studied all of the cuts and bruises on Paul's face. "I had no other choice, Paul," she said. She cleared her throat. "I lo…"

"Suzie, you want to fill me in on what happened here?" Jason interrupted. "I'm going to have a lot to answer for."

Paul stared at her for a long moment. "What were you saying, Suzie?"

"I need to know what happened," Jason interrupted again. "The coast guard, Parish PD, and medics are on their way. I'd like to have some clue as to what to tell them when they get here."

Suzie nodded and glanced away from Paul, though she still held his hand tightly. Between the two of them they explained what had actually happened.

"I had no idea that Trent was involved with drugs," Paul explained. "Once we were out to sea and we were about to dock he put a gun to my head and told me to turn back the way we had come. He had originally planned to pick up more drugs but he saw two men that he was trying to avoid at the dock. He wanted to go back, get the drugs from where he had stashed them, and make it out of town before they even knew he was missing. But when we reached the marina, these two men were waiting for us there. They boarded the boat. They killed Trent for trying to cross them, and I pretended to be his partner to stay alive. I've been leaving clues everywhere I could, but I didn't really think anyone would find them."

"I did," Suzie said softly. She took the seashell out of her pocket and pressed it into Paul's palm.

"I knew where to look. I found the log book, too."

"You're amazing," Paul said. "But I never expected you to put your life in danger like that." He was about to say something more when the medics arrived.

"Go get checked out," Jason insisted.

"Please, Paul," Suzie asked with concern.

Paul frowned and reluctantly let go of Suzie's hand. He held the shell tightly as he walked over to the medics.

"I'm so glad you got my text," Suzie said as she turned to face Jason.

"What text?" Jason asked with a frown. "I didn't get any."

"Then how did you know I was here?" Suzie asked with surprise.

"Mary told me what you were up to," Jason explained. "She knew that you would try and find Paul. I had a little difficulty finding this place, I'm sorry I wasn't here sooner."

"I'm just glad you came," Suzie said with a slight blush rising in her cheeks. "I don't know what I would have done if you hadn't shown up."

"That's why you shouldn't have gone off on your own in the first place," Jason reminded her sternly.

"I know, I know," Suzie agreed. "But I couldn't stand thinking of Paul being injured or trapped somewhere."

"Believe it or not, I do understand," Jason said. "I'm just glad Paul is safe and all of this is going to be cleared up."

The medics finally finished looking Paul over.

"You really should go to the hospital to be checked out," one of the medics said.

"I'm not going anywhere," Paul said gruffly. "I'm fine. Just a little roughed up."

The medic nodded and reluctantly released

him.

"I'm officially a free man," Paul said with a warm smile as he walked over to them.

"Are you sure that's wise, Paul?" Suzie asked with concern as she studied the cuts and bruises on his face.

"Well," Paul hesitated a moment and looked into her eyes. "I did have to promise them that I had someone to look after me."

"You certainly do," Suzie smiled and hugged him gently.

"Your boat is going to have to be searched," Jason interjected. "I can give you both a ride back to Dune House on the police boat."

Paul met Jason's eyes and for a long moment the tension brewed between them.

"Are you sure you don't mind?" he asked as he studied Jason.

"Not at all," Jason replied. "Suzie, when

you're ready?" he nodded lightly at her and walked back towards the Parish police boat that was arriving.

"They're going to tear up my baby," Paul sighed as he passed his gaze over his boat.

"Paul, are you really okay?" Suzie asked as she took his hand in hers.

"Not really," he admitted with a deep frown. "Trent might have been a criminal, but he was still just a kid. He got himself into a mess, and I couldn't help him out of it. Besides that, I hired him. What does that say about my judgment?" he asked.

"It says that you're willing to take a chance," Suzie said softly. "Even on a lost cause. It shows just how much you care."

"Maybe I just saw myself in him," he admitted quietly. "I used to be such a wanderer. Sometimes I used to go out on the boat for weeks at a time."

"So, what has changed?" Suzie asked as she

gently touched his cheek, avoiding the bandage that covered one of the cuts on his face.

"Now, I have someone to come home to," he whispered as he looked into her eyes. "Now, it's hard to stay out on the water without you. Suzie, when that man held a gun to my head, all I could think of was getting home to you."

"Oh Paul, I have something I have to tell you," Suzie said and cleared her throat. "Paul I lo..."

"So, where are the drugs?" Officer Brown barked, interrupting Suzie again.

"My best guess is that they are in Dune House," Paul said with a frown.

"I'll need to get a warrant," Officer Brown sighed as he passed his gaze over Suzie. Suzie might have been mistaken, but she thought she noted a sense of admiration in his eyes.

"No, you won't," she said. "You're welcome to search Dune House for the drugs. I ask that you be respectful that we do have guests. I'm sure that if Trent hid the drugs they must have been in the room where he was staying, as the only time he left it was for breakfast."

"We'll do our best not to cause a commotion," Officer Brown replied. "As for you, Paul, I'm glad to discover that your girlfriend was absolutely right about you the entire time," he offered his hand to Paul. Paul stared at it for a long moment, and then reached out and shook it.

"I'm sure you were just doing your job," Paul said humbly. He wound an arm around Suzie's waist. "Now, if you don't mind, I'd like to head back to the mainland and get some rest."

"There will be some paperwork we'll need you to do. You can give your statement to Officer Allen on the way back to Garber," Officer Brown said with a small smile. "I think you've earned a little flexibility."

Suzie was surprised by the change in the officer's demeanor. She realized that he had never had anything out for Paul personally, but had been too blind to see anything but the obvious. She nestled close to Paul, careful not to put too much pressure on him, but reveling in the warmth of his grasp. All at once the reality of what had almost happened struck her. She began to shiver, and tears built in her eyes.

"You're safe, Paul," she murmured as she turned her face against him to hide her tears.

"I had to get home to you, Suzie," he replied warmly. "Let's go home," he added as he guided her slowly towards Jason's boat.

Chapter Twelve

During the ride back to Dune House, Paul went over the story once more. He held Suzie close, trailing his fingers through her hair. Neither of them would let go of the other for longer than a moment. When they docked at the marina, Paul helped her off the boat.

"When do you think I'll get my boat back?" he asked Jason.

"It may be a few days," Jason said. "It will need to be processed. I'm sorry for the inconvenience."

"It's no trouble," Paul said softly. "It's a good excuse to stick to land for a while."

Jason nodded. "Let me give you a ride back to Dune House," he offered.

"No," Paul shook his head. "It's a lovely evening, we can walk. If you don't mind, Suzie?" he asked. From the warmth in his eyes Suzie could tell that he just wanted to be alone with her. She smiled at the thought and nodded. As they walked from the marina towards Dune House, Paul held her hand firmly in his own.

"Now, what was it you said you had to tell me?" he asked.

Suzie smiled nervously. It had seemed so easy to say it before. She was struggling to get the courage up to speak the words. The sun was setting, painting the sky beautiful shades. They had reached the section of beach in front Dune House. Suzie could see a young couple walking further down the beach. She presumed they were the guests staying the night at Dune House. They were holding hands, and nestled close, just like Paul and her. She stopped and turned to face him. He looked into her eyes knowingly.

"I'm patient," he reminded her in a whisper.

"Paul, when I thought I would never see you again..."

"That will never happen," he assured her. He took both of her hands in his. "Forgive me, Suzie, but I can't wait any longer," he said before meeting her lips with his own. The kiss was slow and sensual, it sent shivers up and down along Suzie's spine. As their lips parted, the words tumbled from the tip of her tongue as naturally as the waves flowing to the sand.

"I love you, Paul," she said and gazed into his eyes.

"I love you too, Suzie," he replied. "From the moment I met you, and until the end of time," he kissed her again. Suzie forgot about all of her fears. She forgot about losing herself in romance. All she felt was gratitude that she had been given the chance to speak the truth to the man she loved.

"Suzie?" Mary called out from the path that led down to the beach. "Are you two decent?" Suzie pulled away from Paul and went running towards Mary.

"My hero!" Suzie said as she hugged her. "If you hadn't warned Jason about what I was up to, I don't think Paul or I would be here right now."

"Some hero," Mary scoffed. "All I did was cook dinner. Although it is delicious. I hope you're both hungry?" she looked between the two of them.

"Oh yes," Paul said.

"Absolutely," Suzie agreed.

"Finally," Mary laughed. As the three of them walked back towards Dune House, Suzie felt wonderful to finally be heading home. On the porch they met Officer Brown who was stepping out of the house along with some other officers.

"We found the drugs," he informed Suzie. "You were right, they were hidden in Trent's room. It looks like this will be an easy case to wrap up."

"The sooner the better," Paul said as he hugged Suzie around the waist.

"You stay safe," Officer Brown said sternly.

"Are you sure you're not hungry?" Mary asked with a sweet smile. "There's plenty to eat."

"No, ma'am," Officer Brown said respectfully. "I think it's best you have a little peace tonight."

"All right then," Mary nodded.

"Now, I want you to tell me just how you found me," Paul said as he led Suzie into the house. "And, promise me, you will never do it again," he said sternly.

"Sorry, sweetheart," Suzie smiled as she pecked his cheek lightly. "I'd do it a thousand times over, if needed. Bonnie Blue and I can't live without you!"

The End

More Cozy Mysteries by Cindy Bell

Dune House Cozy Mystery Series

Seaside Secrets

Boats and Bad Guys

Treasured History

Hidden Hideaways

Heavenly Highland Inn Cozy Mystery Series

Murdering the Roses

Dead in the Daisies

Killing the Carnations

Drowning the Daffodils

Suffocating the Sunflowers

Books, Bullets and Blooms

A Deadly serious Gardening Contest

Wendy the Wedding Planner Cozy Mystery Series

Matrimony, Money and Murder

Chefs, Ceremonies and Crimes

Bekki the Beautician Cozy Mystery Series

Hairspray and Homicide

A Dyed Blonde and a Dead Body

Mascara and Murder

Pageant and Poison

Conditioner and a Corpse

Mistletoe, Makeup and Murder

Hairpin, Hair Dryer and Homicide

Blush, a Bride and a Body

Shampoo and a Stiff

Cosmetics, a Cruise and a Killer

Lipstick, a Long Iron and Lifeless

Camping, Concealer and Criminals

Made in the USA
Coppell, TX
23 June 2020